TALISMAN OF FIRE

Guardians of the Circles
A Novella

D J Eastwood

Copyright © 2021 by D J Eastwood

All rights reserved. This book or any portion thereof may not be reproduced or used in any manner whatsoever without the express written permission of the publisher except for the use of brief quotations in a book review.

First Printing, 2021

ISBN: 979-8596910063

www.apprenticetattoo.co.uk

Cover photos by: photosvit at Bigstock, and the author.

Map created by: Dewi Hargreaves.

Get your free book!

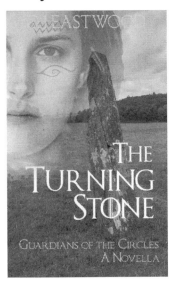

The twin girls that Spirit Messenger Yalta has carried in her belly for so many months come too soon... born dead. She'd hoped that their birth would prompt a proposal of bonding from her lover, Galcar, but he ridicules her for not being able to carry his children.

She runs from her home village in shame, walking the countryside, racked with guilt and tormented by fevers.

When the fever breaks, she has been taken is by Treith, Spirit Master of the great stones of Stanna.

She makes a home there, but the power of the stone circle is failing, and less people come to the solstice gatherings each year. Soon there will not be enough to reposition the turning stone, and change the seasons.

When Treith dies, Yalta is left in charge of the sacred site, and when just a handful of people trickle in to celebrate the solstice, one of them is Galcar, determined to ridicule her once more.

Will she be forced to depart in shame again, or can Yalta rebuild the power of Stanna, and take control of the turning stone?

Go to www.apprenticetattoo.co.uk for more details.

One.

Layne approached the enormous beast, hand outstretched. The matriarch cow snorted and shook her broad head. Sliding her fingers up the long nose, Layne brushed the coarse fringe from the animal's eyes, then ducked under one of the vicious horns, stroking her hand along the flank.

"Hello, Cammy. Are you going to behave for me today?" she whispered.

She pushed on the rump, turning the beast around, so the low morning sun was at her back. Kneeling beside the cow, she placed the urn under her udder and grasped the nearest pair of teats.

Cammy glanced back, dark eye studying Layne for a moment, before returning to chewing her cud.

Layne rested her forehead on the cow's side, breathing in the comforting scent of the animal as the milk splashed into the pot.

"How do you manage her so well?" Geth called from beneath Dubby, a black speckled cow, a few paces away. "She almost kicked me over the last time I tried to milk her."

Layne smiled at her friend, "I talk to her. She knows her name, just whisper it to her and stroke her."

"Where's Albyn?" Geth asked.

Layne switched to the back teats. "Don't know, I haven't seen him this morning."

"He likes you."

"I'm promised to Spirit Messenger Gelyn."

"Mmm, shame," Geth muttered.

Layne patted the cow, then stood and hefted the pot of milk to her shoulder. Geth picked up her own container, and they headed for the village.

They left the pots of milk in the house, ready to make cheese later, and Geth went to find her mentor, Song Keeper Darla.

She found the woman in the Temple, working on a vast cowhide map. Geth watched the bold brushstrokes as Darla hummed the tune of a journey song.

"Can I help you?" Geth asked.

"Hmm? Oh, no. Tomorrow, we will learn the song for this journey. For today, help in the fields or something," she said, waving the girl away.

Geth had come to the Bridge Clan of the Drogga people, along with her brother, Albyn, a year past. Their home tribe, the Joda, lived on the small islands to the north, but opportunities to train were few there. With her sweet voice, Geth had always wanted to become a song keeper, holding the histories of the tribes and learning journey songs used when the clans travelled away from their homes.

She ducked through the low doorway of Spirit Master Boala's house, the place she and Albyn called home at the Bridge Clan. She found her brother straining an amber liquid through a linen cloth.

"What're you doing?" she asked, sitting beside him.

Albyn looked up and smiled. "Mila's baby has a cough," he said, adding honey to the potion. "This will calm it and help her sleep."

"It's a lovely day. Can we go to the beach?" Geth asked.

Boala peered over Albyn's shoulder. "What is in the potion?" he asked.

Peppermint, willow bark, coltsfoot and honey," Albyn said, pouring the liquid into a cup.

"Good, very good," the spirit master said, nodding. "We will study beach and shore plants this afternoon. You may come too, Geth. Bring gathering baskets."

Geth jumped to her feet and clambered up one of the support poles of the house. She searched the storage platform, soon locating three small baskets.

"Catch!" she shouted, dropping them to Albyn.

"Brat," he said, catching two, as the third tumbled to the floor.

"Be careful," Gelyn muttered, head bent over the herbs he was crumbling.

"Are you coming to the beach with us?" Geth asked him as she dropped from the roof timbers.

"I want to finish this," Gelyn said, not looking up.

"You may join us and learn more healing lore," Boala said, pulling a cloak over his shoulders.

"No, I'll stay here."

Boala shrugged and took the potion Albyn had prepared. "I'll deliver this and catch you up," he said.

* * *

Geth scurried along, trying to keep up with Albyn's long stride. He was three years older than her sixteen summers, and a good head taller than her. She glanced at the intricate tattoos around his right eye, the marks of his rank as a spirit messenger, plant keeper and lore keeper. Song keepers had no such marks of rank, though most wore songbird feathers plaited into a braid of hair to show their calling.

"You like Layne, don't you?" Geth asked.

"She is clever, and pretty," Albyn said, glancing at Geth. "She is promised to Gelyn, though."

"He's so boring," Geth said, giggling. Albyn's laughter joined her own as he shoved her shoulder.

"He is a spirit messenger, you should show him some respect," Albyn said, still chuckling.

"What has amused you two?" Boala asked as he caught up with the two youngsters.

"Geth was making fun of your other spirit messenger," Albyn said.

Boala gave Geth a stern look, but was unable to keep the charade up and grinned. "He is a good pupil, but he is rather dull, isn't he?" he said.

Geth pulled off her moccasins at the beach, and hung them around her neck. She followed Boala and Albyn for a while, but got bored with the endless list of plant uses and wandered off to paddle in the warm sea.

The sun was setting by the time they made their way back to the village. Boala went to check on the sick baby, while Geth headed for the house.

"Take the baskets, Geth," Albyn said, passing her the gathered herbs, "I'll only be a while."

She clutched the gathering baskets to he chest as her brother walked around to the back of the house. She heard a giggle, Layne's giggle, as she stepped inside.

* * *

"Shh!" Layne said, pulling Albyn behind the wood pile. Her arms reached around his neck and her lips met his.

Albyn pulled away, peering around to see if they were being watched. "This is dangerous, Layne," he said. "Hafyn promised you to Gelyn. He would be livid if you broke that promise."

"I want to choose my own mate, not take one of my father's choosing," she said, lips pressing to his again.

Albyn clutched her slim body to him. "That is not possible, without your father losing face. He may insist you bond with Gelyn even if you refuse."

"Take me away," she said, burying her face in his chest, "North to your own people."

"They know of your promise to Gelyn," Albyn said.

"South then, to the Great Island."

Albyn held her at arms length, taking in her flushed face framed by her silky brown hair. Her breathing was rapid, and her wide eyes begged.

"You really mean it?"

"Yes. Get us away from here. I want to be your mate, not Gelyn's."

"Let me think on it," Albyn said, stroking her cheek. "Now go home for evening meal, before you're missed."

Layne pressed herself to him, seeking his mouth again. Albyn had no doubt that she was sincere, but did he dare encourage the breaking of a bonding promise?

* * *

Geth strained the cheese curds through a basket of grass, pressing them into a pot to mature for a few days. She took the whey out to a wooden trough, almost getting knocked aside as the pigs smelled the treat, fighting each other to get their head in first.

"Help me with this hide, Geth," Layne called. She was struggling to tie a fresh cow hide to a frame for curing. Geth set her pot aside and helped with the lacings that would stretch the skin tight.

"Are you working on this now?" Geth asked.

"No, they are," Layne said, beckoning to two young boys. She gave each a flint blade and showed them how to scrape away the flesh clinging to the hide. "Don't cut through the hide, of my father will box your ears," she said, "And don't cut yourselves, either."

The boys chattered as they set about the task, and Geth retrieved her pot as Layne followed her towards the spirit master's house.

"What are you doing now?" Geth asked.

"I'm going to the shore for seaweed," Layne said. "Father wants more fertiliser for the fields."

"Want me to come?" Geth asked.

"No," Layne said. "I mean – I can manage by myself."

Geth was about to enter the spirit master's house when she spotted Layne dropping a small pack into her willow creel. She hoisted the basket onto her back and, with a furtive glance around, headed out of the village.

Geth waited until she was out of sight, then followed.

* * *

Albyn sat in the sun, back to a rock, whittling at a piece of driftwood with his flint blade. The salt tang of the sea and the squeal of the gulls made him content. He'd grown up on an island like this, though it was smaller and further north. He couldn't imagine ever being far from the sea.

Albyn caught movement from the corner of his eye and smiled as Layne clambered down between the boulders and onto the beach. He waved as she stood, looking about. She ran to him, flinging her arms around his neck.

"Ready?" he asked.

"Yes. Let's go." She pecked him on the lips, and her face took on a serious cast. "I cannot stay here and break my promise to Gelyn, but he is so dull. I would die if I became his mate."

"We'll go south, to the Great Island, you and me," Albyn said, lifting her up and spinning her around. "Do you have your belongings?"

Layne slipped the basket from her shoulders, pulling her pack from it. "Yes. Father will be disappointed in me," she said, "and Gelyn will be livid."

"Geth will miss me too," Albyn said, heading to the top of the beach.

Three boats lay upturned above the high-water mark, and they rolled the smallest right-side up. Albyn slotted the mast into its holder, fitted the boom and attached the brown linen sail.

He and Layne hauled the vessel down the steep slope of the beach, stopping as the bow touched the water.

"You're sure of this?" Albyn asked.

"Certain."

A wide grin spread across his face as he hauled the craft into the surf. Layne clambered aboard, and he pushed off from the shore and leapt in.

Albyn hauled the sail up the mast and dropped the steering board over the side. His eyes met Layne's, and he grinned. "Layne, daughter of Hafyn, chief of the Bridge Clan of the Drogga tribe. Will you be my bonded mate?"

Layne watched the Isle of Pigs disappearing behind them, then nodded. "Yes, Albyn, Spirit Messenger of the South Clan of the Joda people, yes, I will."

* * *

Geth shielded her eyes against the glare of the late morning sun and watched her best friend and her only brother vanish into the distance. She wiped away a tear with the back of her hand and picked up Layne's basket. She dragged it to the high-water mark and began filling it with seaweed.

* * *

The sun was at its height as the craft skimmed across the glittering water. Albyn took Layne's hand as they watched gulls wheeling above High Island to their right.

"A boat – no, two," said Layne, pointing to their left.

Albyn watched as the vessels turned towards them. He tacked, trying to get ahead of the speeding craft, but the pursuers had larger sails. Each boat held five or six people, and he could see they were armed.

"They don't look friendly," Layne said. "That's the Isle of Eagles, isn't it?"

"Yes, the Eagle Tribe are no friends of the Drogga people," Albyn said, trying one last time to outmanoeuvre them.

"Lower your sail," a voice shouted from the leading boat.

"We have no business with the Eagle Tribe," Albyn called, as the craft drew nearer.

"You are in our waters. That is our business." The man was standing, spear poised, gripping the mast with his other hand.

"We are on our way to the Great Island," Layne called out. "Just passing."

"You should have passed the other side of High Island. Now, drop your sail."

Albyn was glancing around, wondering if there was any way to outrun them, when an arrow thudded into the hull. He unfastened the rope, and the sail clattered down.

"What do you want with us?" he asked, as the Eagle Tribe warriors secured a line to the bow post of their boat.

"The King will want to speak with you, Drogga pigs," one warrior said, sneering.

* * *

Geth limped back towards the village, the full milk pot sloshing its contents as it bumped against her bruised thigh. Dubby had stood while Geth milked her, but Cammy had waited until she finished, then had kicked out. She'd saved the milk from being spilt, but the blow had bruised her leg.

"What is wrong with you?" Darla asked as she hobbled into the house.

"Cammy," Geth said. Darla nodded, everyone in the village knew the bad-tempered cow.

"Doesn't Layne milk her? She's her father's cow."

"She's nowhere to be found," Geth said, covering the milk pot.

"Oh?" Boala said, sitting at the fire with a bowl of porridge, "And where is your brother?"

"I haven't seen him since yesterday," Geth said.

"Well, there's a boat missing from the south beach. Weren't you out collecting seaweed yesterday?"

"I was at the north beach, I saw nothing. Why?"

"Hafyn is furious. It seems his daughter has broken a promise of bonding and gone off with Albyn."

Geth's eyes wandered to Gelyn, sitting on the edge of his bed, head in hands.

The clan chief stormed in at that moment, standing in front of Geth, fists clenched at his sides. "Where are they?" he yelled.

Geth felt her face flush. "I don't know, I just heard about it."

"You are my daughter's best friend, and *he* is your brother. You must know where they are. Tell me."

Boala stood from his breakfast, facing the chief. "She showed genuine surprise when I mentioned it, Hafyn. If what you fear is true, they kept it from everyone."

"Pah," Hafyn said, striding out of the door.

"Do you know where they are?" Boala asked.

"I have no idea," Geth said, hoping they were safe, somewhere.

Two.

Sharp stones dug into Albyn's feet as he and Layne were herded towards the village. The warriors had bound their hands and taken their shoes, prodding them with spear-butts into a square house at the centre of the settlement.

"Bow," said the warrior behind them.

"What do you mean…" Albyn began. The spear butt to the side of his head silenced him.

"Bow to Orenath, Warrior King of the Eagle Tribe," said a voice from the back of the house. Albyn blinked a few times, trying to adjust his eyes to the dark, as he lowered his head.

"Who are you?"

Albyn looked up to find a tall warrior dressed in leather armour. At his side stood a spirit master. He went to extend his hands in greeting, but they were bound together.

"I am Albyn, Spirit Messenger of the South Clan of the Joda people."

"A north islander, eh? And you?" the king asked Layne.

"I am Layne, daughter of Hafyn of the Bridge Clan of the Drogga," she said, glaring at the king.

Orenath smirked. "A chief's daughter? You may be valuable to us after all. So, what did you come to steal?"

"We had no plans to visit your island," Albyn said, "We were headed for the Great Island."

Orenath looked to one of the warriors.

"They were in the waters to the west, between us and High Island, Majesty."

"Well, any sailor of the Drogga would know not to trespass and would have gone west of High Island. So you are not what you claim. Set them to work building the new tomb."

"Wait. Are we to be held here?" Albyn asked.

The warrior dragged him outside by the cord binding his hands. "You are to work," he said grinning. "You are to be slaves."

* * *

The slaves had toiled all afternoon in the day's heat, ripping everything from rubble to enormous slabs from the quarry using wooden wedges. Albyn and Layne loaded the smaller stones into baskets and carried them to the site on a nearby hill.

"How are you coping?" Albyn whispered to Layne when they took a break for water.

"Sore," she said, showing him her bloodied hands. She had never done more challenging work than weeding or hoeing crops before. Albyn ripped a strip from his shirt and bound the hand that was bleeding the most.

"We must get away from here," he whispered.

"Good luck with that," said a voice beside them. Albyn turned to find a man who'd been working in the quarry, and a young woman, bone-thin, a rubble basket lying at her feet.

"Who are you," Albyn asked.

"Roreth. I'm a fisher from the south of the Isle of Pigs. This is my daughter, Geeta."

"Why are you here?" Layne said.

"We were fishing. They," he nodded to the guards, "said we were in their waters and dragged us here."

"So you've tried to escape?" Albyn asked.

"No. We've seen what they do to those that try, though. Don't even think of it."

"Back to work!" roared a voice. The guard walked among them, using a stick to encourage those that were slow to rise.

He raised the weapon to strike Layne as she struggled to her feet. Albyn's hand shot out to stop the blow. The guard rounded on him, bringing the stick down on his shoulder instead. Albyn fell back, clutching at the arm.

"No food for this one tonight," the guard called to his fellow captor. He turned to Albyn, a humourless smile on his lips. "Now, get back to work."

* * *

True to his word, the guard made sure Albyn got nothing that evening after work. Layne sat beside him, eating her own food, then passed the remains of the meal to him.

"No, it's yours," he said.

"Eat," Layne insisted. "You need your strength."

The grey mush was some kind of porridge, cold, with a sour smell, as if they had made it days ago. He forced it down, then took the waterskin.

"Sleep now," said the guard, "You start at dawn." He pushed the roundhouse door closed, and there was the clatter of a beam being dropped outside, trapping the twenty slaves inside.

Layne found Albyn in the dark and pulled him down onto the hard floor beside her. He wrapped her in his arms.

"We'll find a way out," he said.

"I know," she whispered, as exhaustion overtook her and she slept.

* * *

Breakfast had been more of the cold porridge. It seemed that was all the Eagle Tribe was going to feed them. The sun was clearing the horizon as the slaves were marched back to the quarry and started their endless trips back and forth.

It was mid morning when Layne's foot slipped on a rock and the basket of stones tumbled from her back, strewing the contents across the path. The guard was there in moments, lashing Layne's back with his stick.

"Get up, stupid pig," he shouted.

Albyn rushed over, holding the man's arm as he went to strike again. The second guard was on him in moments, beating him with his club. The two of them laid blow after blow on Albyn's body as he curled into a ball.

"Stop!" Layne begged them. A back-handed blow silenced her, but they stopped, kicking his limp body aside.

"Pick up this mess," the guard said, panting and pointing to the spilt load. Layne scrambled to obey, gathering the rocks back into her basket and lifting it to her shoulder again. She glanced down at the lifeless form of her love, begging the spirits not to take him yet.

Albyn coughed and rolled onto his back, opening an eye. Blood poured from his battered nose, but he tried to smile at Layne as she struggled up the slope towards the tomb site.

It took a while before Albyn could haul himself to his feet. He picked up his basket and hobbled back towards the quarry.

Layne touched his hand as they passed on the laborious treks back and forth, and when they got water and a break, she bathed his bruises and scrapes as best she could.

There was more of the foul porridge that evening, and they again curled up together to sleep.

* * *

"Nightshade," Albyn whispered as they passed the tall plants growing beside the tomb site.

"What of it?" Layne asked.

"Pull a few leaves as you pass, I'll do the same. Don't touch your mouth until the break, when we can wash our hands."

Layne nodded, snatching two of the leaves, and tucking them into her pouch.

"What are they for?" Layne asked as they sat on the broken rock of the quarry for their break. Albyn poured water onto his hands, washing them, then nodded for Layne to do the same.

"If we can gather enough, they may get us out of here," he said.

They sorted their harvest in the dark of the roundhouse that night, Albyn tucking the leaves into the thatch above their heads.

"How much will we need," Layne asked.

"More than this," Albyn said. "We'll collect more tomorrow."

* * *

Two days later, Albyn decided that they had enough of the deadly plant. They set off for the tomb, as usual, but were halted mid-morning and taken back to the village centre. Layne gasped when a party walked into the village, leading two Eagle Tribe men by their bound hands. The man in the lead was her father, Hafyn, and the second was Gelyn, her once promised mate.

Hafyn made elaborate introductions with Orenath, each trying to outdo the other in making themselves look the superior tribe.

"I have two foolish raiders who tried to steal cattle from the south of our island," Hafyn said, nodding towards the red-faced captives. "We will return them in exchange for some Drogga people I believe you have captive."

Albyn watched Gelyn as his gaze searched the ragged party of slaves, his eyes coming to rest on Layne. He whispered into Hafyn's ear, and the chief looked up at his daughter.

"We have a few of your people that have violated our boundaries," Orenath said. "One may particularly interest you. I believe she is your daughter."

Hafyn glared at the Eagle Tribe king. "I have two sturdy sons," he said, "But I have no daughters. I am told you have kidnapped a fisher named Roreth, and his daughter. If you are agreeable to the trade, we will take them."

Orenath looked stunned for a moment, then smiled at Hafyn.

"That is acceptable." He turned to the guards. "Free the fisher and his daughter."

The two captives walked towards Hafyn, Roreth clasping his hand and thanking the chief. They led the two Eagle Tribe men over to the slaves. No one cut their bonds.

"We thank you, King Orenath," Hafyn said, turning to leave the village.

Albyn watched tears streaming down Layne's face, her shoulders shaking, as her father walked away.

"Stupid fools," Orenath shouted as he approached the bound warriors, striking each one across the face. "You disgrace our tribe with your pointless raid. You will work as slaves for a moon, then we will see if you are still fit to be warriors."

They took the slaves back to the quarry, and Albyn took Layne's hand.

"He has disowned me," she whispered.

"I'm sorry," Albyn said, squeezing her rough fingers.

"We have to get away," Layne said. "Soon."

"We will, my love. We will."

Three

In the grey light before sunrise, Albyn gathered the nightshade leaves from the thatch. He tucked them into his pouch, tying it closed.

"Tonight," he whispered to Layne as she sat up, rubbing sleep from her eyes. He took her calloused hand in his own, kissing it. "We will get away, go to the Great Island, and start a new life, together."

A livid scar marred the perfect skin of her forehead, now, but her smile still made him melt, her hazel eyes glistening with tears. "Together," she said.

* * *

The tomb was progressing, and the inner walls were complete. The intricate task of constructing the corbelled roof was next, and the larger stones were soon laid. Each circuit of the round chamber saw the stones pulled in a hand's-breadth more, creating an upturned cone.

Layne had been told to pass the stones up to the builder, balanced on a flimsy platform set up around the chamber. Albyn was with a team bringing rubble to backfill the roof.

They sat together during a break, whispering plans for their escape. Roreth, the fisherman, had told them that the Eagle Tribe kept boats at a beach to the south end of the island, and they planned to go there, steal a small craft, and cross the narrow stretch of water to the Great Island.

"When we finish work, they always ask for someone to fill the water skins," Albyn said. "I'll volunteer, then poison the water in each one."

"Be careful," Layne said, as their guards called them back to work.

* * *

"The ceiling is getting too high," Albyn said as he tipped his basket of rubble.

The builder glared at him. "I am in charge here," he said. "Keep your stupid opinions to yourself, unless you want a beating."

Albyn studied the building. The unsteady construction relied on the weight of the rubble and stones on the outside to stabilise it. Still, the ceiling was rising faster than the slaves could bring in the increasing amounts of fill needed to reinforce it. He shouldered his basket and headed for the quarry.

Halfway back with the next load, Albyn heard a rumble, followed by screams and shouts. He dropped his basket, running up the hill towards the tomb as a cloud of dust rose from its centre.

"Layne!" he yelled, sprinting to the tomb entrance and crawling along the narrow passageway.

The dust choked him as he emerged into the central chamber. A section of the ceiling had collapsed, smashing onto the platform. The builder lay to one side, neck twisted at an impossible angle. Albyn screamed Layne's name as he searched through the rubble. He spotted her head protruding from under a pile of stone.

"I'll get you out, Layne. Just hold on," he said, throwing the stones aside as fast as he could. He glanced at her pained face and saw her shake her head. Her lips were moving. Albyn dropped to his knees beside her.

Her eyes were wide with fear as he leant closer to hear her. She coughed, and a gout of blood dribbled from her mouth.

"I… love… you," she whispered, then her eyes lost their focus. Her spirit had gone.

Albyn wailed, then scrabbled at the stones covering her broken body. Hands grasped at his arms, dragging him from her. He fought them for a moment, then allowed them to pull him away, his chest heaving with his sobbing, eyes blinded by tears.

* * *

Albyn was numb. A day had passed, unnoticed by him, and the two bodies now lay on the ground, both covered in white linen. The spirit master walked a circuit of them, calling to the ancestors and the spirits to take them to their loved ones. He nodded to the warriors, and the men lifted the bodies, carrying them away for the sky-burial. The women remained, wailing the ritual chants. The rites had been the same for both the builder and for Layne. Starved and beaten in life, it was as if she had acquired value in death. He stood and followed, watching as they laid her body out atop the high wooden platform for the birds to strip.

Somehow he was back in the dilapidated roundhouse. They placed a bowl of the rancid gruel in front of him, but he pushed it away. Eager hands snatched it at once.

They expected him to work and, when he showed no inclination to do so, they beat him. Albyn wondered if they might kill him, then he could cross the death river to be with Layne again.

He regained consciousness, aching and bleeding, realising that he was still on the Isle of Eagles, a captive and still alive.

He trudged back and forth from the quarry to the tomb, the basket on his back. The blows to hurry him were frequent, but he barely felt them. The pain in his heart was far worse.

Albyn lay awake at nights, wondering how he could have prevented this. It had been Layne's idea to run away together, but he had soon come round to the plan. He'd never dared ask for advice on the boat crossing, for fear of word getting back to Layne's father. If only they'd sailed around High Island.

After a few days, he ate the food again, shovelling it into his mouth without thought. He considered trying to escape, but what was the point.

The tomb was nearing completion now, and they had moved some of the slaves on to farm work. He continued carrying stone, though. Basket after basket, all tipped onto the huge hollow mound.

* * *

They had given Albyn the task of sweeping the last of the dust from the finished tomb. The small shell lamp burned in a niche in the wall as he worked his way around the chamber with the birch-twig brush. He kept the light at his side as he swept the debris along the entrance tunnel. As he approached the daylight once more, there were voices outside the tomb.

"The bones of the dead are ready, King Orenath. Shall we inter them in the tomb?" the spirit master asked.

"Bring the bones of the builder, Marev, here," he said.

"And the girl?"

"Throw those in the sea," the king said, "She was nothing but a slave."

Albyn bit his tongue to stop himself crying out. Layne deserved to have her bones laid in the tomb she had died for, as much as the arrogant builder.

He checked that the king and the spirit master had moved on before he stepped out into the sunlight.

Sleep didn't come that night, and Albyn lay thinking of the king's words. His hatred of the man grew as he reasoned that he and Layne had been no threat to the Eagle Tribe, and there had been no real reason to enslave them. If only Hafyn had taken Layne back in exchange for the warriors he traded, she, at least, would be alive and safe. He felt for the pouch, forgotten at his belt all this time. It still bulged with the dried nightshade leaves, and he began to form a plan.

Four.

Albyn spent the night grinding the nightshade leaves to a powder with two stones. He tipped the poison back into the pouch, getting a little sleep before dawn.

It was so tempting to tell the others about his plan, but he did not know who he could trust. As the workday drew to a close, he volunteered to fill the water skins. The guard followed him to the river, sitting on the bank upstream, whittling at a piece of wood.

Albyn pulled the stoppers on the skins, dropping a pinch of poison into all but one. He filled them, sealed them, and hung each one over his shoulder. Rinsing his hands, he called to the guard, and they set off towards the village.

Each house received a full waterskin, Albyn reserving the last one for the slave house.

* * *

In the pitch dark of his prison, no one stirred. Albyn prised the mud from the rotting laths and broke a small hole in the back wall. He checked for movement in the house, then ripped more away. Soon, there was a hole big enough to squeeze through. The night was cloudy, and he crept around the house by the light of the dying fire outside. The guard lay by the door. Albyn wondered if he was dead. Nightshade was a poison dependent on dose, and the guard had been in the scorching sun all afternoon. He'd have drunk a lot. Just as he approached, the man stirred, his hand going to his forehead as he looked about in confusion.

"Who's that?" he slurred, struggling to focus on Albyn. The stone from the hearth made a sickening crunch as Albyn brought it down on his head, and he slumped back against the wall. Tears blurred his eyes as he remembered when this man had beaten Layne, and the rock fell again, smashing into the side of his head. Blood, black in the firelight, dribbled from his ear as he toppled to the side.

Albyn dropped the stone and turned towards the king's house. The door was ajar, and he could hear a voice from inside, muttering curses. He peered in, finding a woman sitting on the edge of a bed, flailing her arms at some unseen foe. The fire still blazed in the hearth, and he crept inside, looking for the king. Leant against the back wall, he found the pack he had brought. He checked inside, finding his cape, a spare tunic, and his knife. The noise startled him, and he whirled around, blade in his hand.

"How are you here?" the king asked. He was clutching at his head, as if in pain. "I killed you in battle, Redovar, you are dead."

Albyn's arm slipped around the man's neck as he staggered forward. The knife blade drew blood as he struggled to free himself.

"Who do you think I am?" Albyn asked.

"Redovar, my brother. I killed you…"

"I am not Redovar, I am Albyn. You enslaved my intended, Layne and me for no good reason, and now she is dead."

"The slave is dead. The slave is dead," Orenath whispered, over and over.

"And now, you will die," Albyn said. He would have preferred to see fear in his eyes, not listen to the deranged ramblings of the king's drugged nightmares, but he would have his revenge.

The jagged edge sliced open the flesh of his throat, and his whispers became a scream, then a bubbling gurgle as blood poured into his airway.

Albyn dropped the twitching body to the floor, throwing his blade beside it. His gaze caught the intricate necklace at the king's throat. Hollow eagle bones, interspersed with curved, black talons. He drew the king's ornamented knife from his belt, slicing the cord, and pushed the trinket into his pouch. Stepping over the corpse, he made for the door. A rustle above his head made him look up. There, perched on a beam, was a sea eagle. The bird was old, with ragged plumage. Albyn wrapped a sleeping fur over his arm and clambered onto a stool. The bird put up little resistance as he untied the cord restraining it and pulled it onto his wrist, carrying it out of the house. The eagle stepped onto a drying rack beside the door, regarding Albyn with interest. He didn't know if the elderly creature would survive, but it had more chance outside.

In the village, all was quiet. He wondered how many would perish from the poison, but with Layne gone, he couldn't bring himself to care.

Pulling the heavy beam from the slave house entrance, he threw open the door.

"The guard is dead," he said, as people stirred. "Make your getaway now, if you wish."

"Where would we go?" a woman asked.

"I'm told there are boats at the south end of the island. Make your way to the Great Island."

"What of the villagers?" someone asked.

"I have drugged them. Do not drink from any water skins but this one," Albyn said, pointing to the skin by the door. "Good luck."

"Will you not come with us?" a man said, peering outside.

"I have other plans. Be quick now."

The slaves crept outside, wary of Albyn's words. Most glanced at the guard, blood pooled around his head, beside the door.

Albyn watched the slaves melt away into the night, then lifted his pack to his shoulder. He scavenged in a few houses, finding bread and cheese, then turned north.

"What will become of me, Spirit Messenger?" said a voice behind him. He turned to find a lad, eyes fixed on his.

"Are you alone?" Albyn asked. The boy nodded. He'd seen the child working, but had assumed he was with a parent. It sickened him they kept child slaves at all, but one so young, alone…

"What is your name?"

"Amalan, son of Breen. Father was killed when they captured us."

"And your people?"

"Poan Tribe. Father was a trader. The Eagle Tribe took his boat and his goods, then kept me here."

Albyn knelt to the boy's level. "Can you run fast?" he asked.

"Yes, Messenger."

Albyn closed his eyes and sighed, deciding. "Come with me. I have one stop to make before we leave."

Amalan followed him to the house of the spirit master. They crept inside, finding all quiet, just one bed occupied. Albyn grasped the throat of the sleeping man and squeezed.

"What? Who is it?" the old man squeaked. He must have drunk the poisoned water, for his eyes were struggling to focus.

"Where are Layne's bones?" Albyn asked.

"Who?"

"The slave girl that died at the tomb. Where is she?"

"I did as Orenath said. I laid her bones on the beach to the north, for the tide to take."

"When is high tide?" Albyn said. He had not seen the ocean since their capture and had lost touch with the cycles of sea and sky.

There was terror in the spirit master's eyes now. "Before dawn. They… they may still be there."

Albyn gave a back-handed slap to the frightened man, then grasped Amalan by the hand.

"Come, we must hurry," he said.

* * *

Grey was tingeing the sky, enough to see by, as they ran to the beach. The sand stretched away either side of them. Where would her bones be?

"Go left," Albyn said. "We are looking for the bones of Layne."

"Your mate?" Amalan asked.

"We were promised. Hurry now."

The sea had almost reached the band of seaweed along the top of the beach. There may still be time to save her.

"Here, Messenger," Amalan shouted. "Come quick."

A larger wave was rolling in, and Albyn sprinted to the boy. He saw the few remaining bones as the wave broke, diving into the surf, hands grasping at the wet sand. His fingers closed around small bones, and he staggered out of the ebbing wave.

His hand held just two of the wrist bones, the rest had washed away. He pushed them into his pouch and scrambled back into the water, sifting through the sand, hoping to find some other memento of his love. It was useless. Everything else had gone.

Albyn sat, head in hands. Amalan shuffled up beside him.

"I caught this, Messenger, before it was swept away," he said.

There, clutched in the boy's hands, was Layne's skull. Albyn reached for it, a tear in his eye as he cradled the head.

Dark holes stared where bright, hazel eyes had once dwelt, bare teeth where he had kissed soft lips.

"Thank you, Amalan," he said, managing a smile for the lad. "Let's get away from here, before day breaks."

They found a boat upturned at the top of the beach. It was too small to have a sail, but there were paddles wedged inside. Albyn dragged it towards the water, Amalan straining on the second rope. His first good look at his companion made him think the boy could be only ten or eleven summers old. They manoeuvred the craft into the water, then Albyn lifted Amalan in. He pushed off, jumping aboard as the stern floated. The sunrise stained the horizon blood-red as they paddled out of the bay.

Five.

The sky was blue from east to west, the sun strong on their backs as they paddled towards the Isle of Pigs.

It was late afternoon before they were close enough to see a small bay with a beach. They had seen smoke rising from a settlement to the east, but nothing nearby. Albyn put the craft ashore, leaping into the shallow water and lifting Amalan out. They dragged the boat to the top of the beach, turning it over as a shelter. Albyn climbed the steep slope to the clifftop but saw no sign of life.

"Crawl under the boat," he told Amalan, "We'll get some sleep and move on after dark."

"Where are we going, Messenger?" the boy asked.

"The Bridge Clan, north of here."

"Will there be more killing? Revenge?" he asked. His youthful face showed no emotion.

"Yes."

Amalan crawled under the boat and lay back in the sand. "I wish I had avenged my father's death."

"Orenath is dead," Albyn said, following him into the shelter, "Perhaps I have taken your revenge for you."

There was silence, and Albyn wondered if the boy had fallen asleep. He heard a sniff, then a soft sob.

"Thank you, Spirit Messenger," Amalan whispered.

* * *

They moved on at dusk, heading north again in the failing light. There was a crescent moon, and both felt the chill of the evening through their worn clothing. Neither had shoes, but the constant treks back and forth to the quarry had hardened their feet.

They talked as they walked, though Albyn gave away little of his life. Amalan said that he had a mother and a sister, and Albyn vowed to get him back to them, somehow.

As dawn broke, the travellers found an overhanging rock and settled in for the day. The bread Albyn had taken was stale now, and the tiny remnants of the cheese were sweating and greasy. A stream gave drinking water, and they slept the day away.

* * *

"There it is," Albyn said, pointing to the cluster of stone roofed houses on the strip of land between two lakes.

"Do we go in now?" Amalan asked.

"No, dawn is too close. We'll wait for another night."

"There's no food," Amalan said, rubbing his belly.

Albyn glanced around, spotting the speckled black cow twenty paces away. He took out his cup and beckoned to Amalan. The startled cow took a moment to catch, but Albyn knew she was the quietest in the herd. He milked a full cup from her, passing it to his companion. He took a cupful for himself, then another for Amalan.

"That will keep us going for now," he said, leading the way to a beach the tribe seldom used. They settled amongst some boulders and slept.

* * *

The village was silent. Albyn had watched for a long time, checking that they had all gone to sleep, then crept from their hiding place.

"Will you poison them, Messenger?" Amalan asked.

"No. This is my sister's home. I must sneak in to take my revenge. Wait here. If there is trouble – if I don't come back – run to the shore and get yourself wet. Claim you escaped the

Eagle Tribe, and your boat sank. They are better people than the Eagle Tribe… well, most of them are. They will take you in. Do not mention me, I am unpopular here."

"You will return for me, Messenger," Amalan said.

Albyn's first stop was the chief's house. If only that vile man had rescued his daughter, she would be alive today. He crept to the door, easing it open. A flame still flickered in the hearth, and he could make out a body in a bed. He knew that Hafyn's mate had died, but wondered where his two sons were.

He crept around the fire, looking for any movement in the house. There was none.

"So, you return," said a voice from the bed. "Come to beg me to take you and my treacherous daughter back, have you?"

Albyn froze, knife in his hand. He'd hoped to take Layne's father by surprise.

"No."

"What then? Where is Layne?"

"Dead. You killed her when you failed to take her back from the Eagle Tribe."

"Dead? How?" He could hear Hafyn's shock. Albyn needed to keep him unsettled.

"Crushed to death when the tomb we were building collapsed. Your actions led to her death."

"Building? I thought the slaves would do fieldwork, tending animals. I thought it would teach her a lesson and rid her of you."

Albyn stepped closer. "You may as well have killed her yourself."

The speed with which the chief leapt from his bed surprised Albyn, but he dropped to a crouch, knife to the fore.

"Your actions killed her, and I will kill you," Hafyn said, lunging at Albyn with a short spear. It must have been beside the bed for him to arm himself so fast.

Albyn leapt back, slashing with his blade, unable to get close enough to do any damage. The spear jabbed again, catching Albyn's arm. He ignored the pain and reached down, grabbing a handful of hot ashes from the hearth. He flung them into Hafyn's face, following through with the knife. Hafyn clawed at his eyes, dropping the spear and leaving his body unprotected.

There was a gasp as Albyn's knife drove up under his ribs and into his heart, then his body slumped.

"I did not kill her," Albyn said as he lowered Hafyn's body to the floor, "With her last breath, she told me she loved me."

Albyn left the knife embedded in Hafyn's chest and searched his body. The amulet he sought was not there. He looked around the bed, on the table, but could not find it. Well, if it wasn't here, it would be at the temple.

* * *

The temple door was a heavy leather curtain. Albyn eased it aside and peered in. A few smoking beef-fat lamps stood on an altar, casting a low light around the building. Slumped in front of the dying fire sat Gelyn.

The stone from the hearth was hot in his hand as he crept behind the spirit messenger. He brought the rock down on the back of his skull and watched him fall to one side, his head clattering off the flagstone floor.

Albyn found what he was looking for at the centre of the altar. The string of amber beads, known as the Fire Stones, were the badge of office of the clan leaders of the Bridge Clan. He picked them up and slipped them around his neck.

He looked down at Gelyn, the man Layne had abandoned for him. There was still a rise and fall of breath, and Albyn searched his belt for a knife. Remembering he'd left it in Hafyn's chest, he reached for the rock once more. He gripped it with both hands and raised it above his head.

"Don't," said a voice from the doorway. He looked up to find Geth glaring at him. "Don't kill him."

"Why not? He is as guilty as Hafyn of Layne's death."

Geth ran to his side, taking the stone from his hands. "Layne is dead?"

Albyn told the story of their capture, and the exchange of prisoners at the Isle of the Eagles. How Hafyn had disowned her and taken two others instead. He explained the collapse of the tomb that had killed his love, then told of his escape.

"She was like a sister to me," Geth sobbed. "I missed you both so much, when you left."

"I'm sorry," Albyn said, clutching Geth to him. "I took my revenge on Orenath."

"You killed their king?" Geth asked.

"Yes, and I killed Hafyn too."

Geth's hands went to her mouth. "We need to get away from here. They will slaughter you if they catch you now."

"I will go, you stay."

"I am your sister! You need my help, and they'll never believe that I don't know where you've gone, anyway."

Albyn nodded, then looked at Gelyn's body.

"Don't kill him," Geth said, again. "Gelyn suffers enough. He loved Layne and thinks you stole her away from him. He hasn't smiled since the day you left."

Albyn reached down and inspected a stone tablet at Gelyn's throat. A quick tug broke the cord, and he tucked it away with the other amulets.

Albyn asked Geth if she needed to get some belongings, but she shook her head.

"Too much danger of us being discovered, I have what I need," she said, lifting the food offerings from the altar and stuffing them into a linen bag. "Come on."

They crept through the silent village, toward the boundary wall.

Amalan hugged Albyn as he walked through the gate.

"I knew you'd come back," he said.

"Amalan, this is my sister, Geth," Albyn said. "Geth, Amalan was a slave at the Eagle Tribe settlement. I need to get him back to his family. He will come with us."

"Is there any food, Messenger?" the boy asked. Geth smiled and reached into her pack, producing a loaf of bread.

"Share it," she said. "I have eaten today."

Albyn took the lead, and they headed south.

* * *

Albyn, Geth, and Amalan took a boat from the beach, paddling out into the bay before raising the sail. They turned south, tacking against an east wind as the sun rose. Keeping west of the High Island, they glimpsed a half-dozen vessels heading north from the Isle of the Eagles before they rounded the tip of the island.

Six.

The pain woke Gelyn. He struggled to sit up and touched the lump on the back of his head. Someone had attacked him. But who?

He stood, balancing himself with a hand on the altar, noticing the Fire Beads had gone. He picked his way to the door, pulling aside the curtain. It was almost light, and the last traces of red were leaving the eastern sky. A woman waved, and he returned her greeting, then set off for Chief Hafyn's house.

The door was ajar, so the chief must be awake. He knocked and walked in.

"Chief Hafyn. I think we were attacked last night. They knocked me out and…" Gelyn stared at the crumpled body on the floor by the hearth. Darkening blood pooled around the chief, the handle of a knife protruding from his chest.

* * *

"Do you have any idea who hit you?" Spirit Master Boala said.

Gelyn shook his head. "I've no memory of it. I think I drifted off to sleep. When I woke this morning, I had this lump on my head. What about the knife that killed Hafyn?"

The spirit master bent to look at the murder weapon.

"Eagle Tribe," he said. "High born, Eagle Tribe."

"You think…?"

"They have always stolen cattle. I'm sure our own young warriors do likewise, but to kill a chief, that is an act of war."

"Raiders!" came a cry from outside. Gelyn rushed to the door, grabbing the arm of a warrior running past.

"What is it?" he asked.

"Thirty or more raiders. Eagle Tribe warriors," he gasped, "Get the women and children to safety."

Gelyn relayed the information to the spirit master, then ran through the village, gathering the women and children. He herded them into the temple, a place of sanctuary, moving them to the back of the building.

"Is everyone here?" he asked.

"Where is Geth?" a woman said.

"Oh no," Gelyn said, "She planned to go to the stone circle early today to do a ceremony. Let's hope she saw then coming and got away."

* * *

The battle had been short, but fierce. Drogga men outnumbered the Eagle warriors, but they had inflicted a lot of damage. The chief's house had been burnt down, and two Drogga men killed. Many were injured.

The Eagle Tribe had turned and run when their leader died in the battle, chased back to their boats by the Drogga warriors. They left four dead behind.

"Hold still, Valan," Gelyn said, "Once I sew this, you can move then." He placed the stitches with care, closing the gash in the man's arm. "Why did they attack us like this?" he asked.

Valan winced as Gelyn pierced his skin with the bone needle. "The one who attacked me kept shouting, 'Where is the king's amulet? Where is the talon necklace?' I didn't know what to make of it."

"The Eagle Tribe revere the sea eagle," Boala said, checking Gelyn's work. "I know their king wears a talisman made from eagle talons and bone, but why would they think we have it?"

"Perhaps we'll find out when we retaliate," Valan said.

* * *

As their boat cleared the High Island, Amalan climbed back to sit with Albyn.

"Turn west," he said.

Albyn smiled. "Why, we want to reach the shore ahead."

"Because the currents here are faster than the winds," the boy said. "Turn west, and we may reach the point ahead of us now."

Albyn turned the boat, so the rising wind was at their backs. He set the sail, and Amalan tied off the rope.

"You learned from your father, then?"

"He was a skilled sailor, and he taught me much. I remember these waters. The tide can carry you out into the northern ocean if you don't respect its power."

"Then I am lucky I brought you with us," Albyn said as the boy clambered back to the bow, "Thank you, Amalan."

"He's a brave lad," Geth said, sitting beside her brother. Her fingers traced the scars across his face, then touched his nose. "Your face is different… damaged."

Albyn nodded. "Too many beatings, and no treatment apart from a rinse with water." He felt his hooked nose. "There was no one to straighten this, when they broke it."

"They didn't beat Layne… did they?"

"She had her scars too." Tears formed at the corners of Albyn's eyes. "I've killed Orenath and Hafyn. I've killed the brute that beat her, and spirit knows how many I've poisoned with nightshade. Why do I not feel avenged, Geth?"

"I loved her too," she said, "I miss her. Maybe with time it gets easier."

Albyn looked into his sister's eyes, and knew that she didn't believe that any more than he did.

* * *

They made landfall just as the sun set, sailing into a broad bay and beaching on a bank of shingle. Albyn and Geth hauled the boat while Amalan searched for driftwood along the beach. Geth had a fire-bow with her, and they soon got a blaze going.

They used pebbles from the fire to heat a small pot of broth that Geth had grabbed from the temple as they left the Bridge Clan, and they skewered hunks of bread on sticks, toasting it to drive out the stale taste.

"We will need to find a village, or hunt for food tomorrow," Geth said. "We have nothing of value to exchange, but they may keep the travellers pledge."

Most tribes would feed those on a journey, expecting their own to be treated likewise.

"We don't need the boat," Albyn said. "We will travel overland now. Perhaps a coastal clan would trade for it."

"We'll see tomorrow," Amalan said. "I'm tired."

* * *

The voice woke Albyn.

"Hello, the camp!"

He rolled out from beside the boat and climbed to his feet. "Greetings," he called, hands held out in welcome. "We are travellers. We came ashore at dusk."

"Yes, our people saw your fire," the man said. "I am Besson, leader of the Bay Clan of the Cheel people." He waved a hand behind him at a half-dozen men and women. "These are people of my clan. Can we offer you the shelter of our village?"

"That is generous, thank you," Albyn said. He turned as the others joined him. "This is my sister, Geth, a song keeper, and Amalan, of the Poan people. I am Albyn, a spirit messenger of the Joda people."

"How do such distant tribes come to be travelling together?" Besson asked.

"Amalan and I were slaves of the Eagle Tribe," Albyn said, "We escaped and picked up my sister before coming to the

Great Island. We would be happy to trade the boat if it has value to you."

Besson walked around the small vessel, scratching his thick beard. "I could give you a bag of salt for it," he said, glancing at Albyn for a reaction. Albyn was about to accept when Amalan stepped in front of him.

"A bag of salt? Do you insult us, Chief Besson?" he said. "This craft has carried us from the Isle of Pigs. Men with the experience of generations built it."

"Amalan!" Albyn whispered, but the boy waved him back.

"Well," Besson said, stunned by the lad's audacity, "We could add some food for your journey. There's a little rot starting here on the bow."

Amalan poked at the small hole. "A *skilled* man could repair that in half a day," he said, "We have no shelter or weapons, and you would give us a bag of salt?"

"What would you ask, then?" Besson said.

"No, no," Amalan said, turning away. "If it is so worthless, we'll use it as firewood tonight."

"I didn't say it was worthless," Besson said. "Perhaps you would accept some fine blades and some of our dried beef? Maybe a travelling shelter? We would not want to insult our visitors."

"A knife each, an axe, a bow, and a stout spear would be useful, as would a shelter."

Besson nodded.

"And dried beef would be excellent travelling food for us," Amalan said. "We are bound for the Poan lands."

Besson smiled, relieved to have avoided upsetting the visitors. The boat would be a valuable addition to the Bay Clan's fleet. He held out his hands to Amalan. "Do we have a deal?"

Amalan stroked the bow of the vessel, then looked into Besson's eyes. "And the salt," he said.

The leader burst into laughter, reaching to clasp Amalan's hands.

"You drive a hard bargain, trader Amalan. Yes, the salt too."

Amalan smiled for the first time. "You have gained an excellent vessel there, Chief Besson," he said.

"And you have gained every scrap of what it was worth, young man. Now, come and get breakfast with us."

"You bargain well, Amalan," Albyn said, as they followed the Cheel people along the beach.

Amalan grinned. "I am my father's son," he said.

Seven.

The trio spent two days with the Bay Clan. Amalan, being strong and agile, helped to cap the last of the roof on a new house, while Albyn collected herbs for the clan's spirit master.

They left on the third morning, loaded with their newly traded weapons and food.

The summer weather meant long days of travelling, but they made good progress. They left the Cheel people's lands and moved into Atay country. Several villages had welcomed them, but this night saw them camped on the edge of woodland, high in the hills.

"Has Amalan gone to bed?" Albyn asked, glancing at the shelter.

"Yes, the walking is hard on him, but he keeps up with us," Geth said.

"I wish to journey to the lower world," he said. "I had no time to do any ceremony for Layne, and I want to see she is safe in the land of the dead. Will you drum for me?"

"We have no drum, Albyn."

"This will do," he said, rapping his knuckles on the hollow log they were using as a seat.

Geth nodded and searched the woodpile for a stout stick. Albyn sat on the ground, his back against the log, as his sister began a fast rhythm. He closed his eyes and felt himself pulled below.

Albyn was familiar with the lower world, the gateway to the land of the dead. It was never light here, always like dawn, or dusk. There were no colours, only grey. In the distance were the black waters of the death river, marking the boundary between the living and the dead. Those who left the land of the living crossed it to be with the ancestors, but if the living crossed, they would be trapped. Dead too.

He could see a cloaked figure standing on the river bank nearest to him, staring across the dark stream. He started towards the river, then stopped as the air shimmered in front of him and a figure materialised. He was used to seeing ancestors on the far bank, not close enough to touch like this.

"Who are you?" Albyn asked. The face was smeared with red ochre, and the eyes glowed like hot coals.

The voice rasped as if burned dry. "I am the Spirit of Fire, your master, and you will obey me."

"I will not be a slave again," Albyn said.

"You wear the talisman of the fire masters. I will teach you, if you and your people worship me."

"No. I have no business with you," Albyn said, trying to walk around the spirit and reach the river.

"I will have the veneration of you and your people," the spirit shouted, "Bow before me!"

Albyn turned away, but a hand grabbed his arm. He screamed at the burning sensation, smelled the searing of his flesh, then he was back at the camp, watching Geth drumming.

He glanced across at the shelter, then ran towards it. The ox-hide structure, with Amalan still sleeping inside, was on fire. Flames were licking from both ends of their temporary home, and Albyn beat at it with his hands. He was tackled to the ground as cold water splashed on his hands and arms.

"What are you doing?" Geth shouted.

Albyn looked around. It was usual to follow the drumbeat back from the lower world. Being snatched back had disoriented him

"Amalan... the shelter," he said, staring at his blistering hands.

"Amalan is fine," Geth said. "One moment you were sitting, eyes closed, the next you were trying to put the fire out with your bare hands."

Albyn looked across the fire. The shelter was unharmed, and Amalan was peering out to see what the noise was about.

"It was the spirit of fire," Albyn said. "He showed me the shelter. It was on fire, and Amalan was inside it."

Geth poured the last of the water onto her brother's hands. "Why?"

"I don't know, it has something to do with these beads," Albyn said, clutching at the necklace. He winced as the pain from the burns registered in his confused mind.

"Take off your tunic," Geth said. "We have nothing for healing, but I want to see how badly you are hurt."

She inspected his hands, finding the right burned worse than the left, but the blisters around his upper arm puzzled her.

"How did you get these?" she asked.

"The spirit gripped my arm, I felt his hand burning me."

"This was in the lower world?"

Albyn nodded.

"Yet your tunic is undamaged on that sleeve," Geth said, inspecting the garment. "What will treat this?" she asked.

Albyn looked at the plants surrounding them. "Chickweed, and the petals of the dog-roses," he said.

Amalan jumped up, picking the low-growing green leaves, then pulling flowers from the rose bush. Geth found some beef-fat that their last hosts had given them, crushing the lot to a paste. She rubbed it over Albyn's blisters, then sat back.

"What does the spirit of fire want with you, Albyn?"

"It's this necklace," he said. "Do you know anything about fire masters?"

Geth considered for a moment. "Song keeper Darla bound me to secrecy, but I don't suppose it matters now. I stumbled upon a strange rite, one night. All the protected-of-spirit were there, the star master, star keepers, the spirit master, and Chief Hafyn. They were chanting a verse unknown to me, and they had four fires burning at the stone circle. They jumped the fires, then spread out the embers and walked over them in bare feet."

"You saw this?" Albyn said.

Geth nodded. "Darla missed me and came to look for me. She dragged me away but made me swear never to tell of it. She said they worshipped the fire spirit every dark of the moon."

"This is what the fire spirit wants from me. He asked me to bow before him, told me he was my master."

"Take them off," Geth said, reaching for his neck. She untied the cord and slipped the beads into Albyn's pouch. "There, perhaps that will help."

"I hope so," Albyn said.

* * *

Albyn's burns were almost healed by the summer solstice and they celebrated with the Uru people, but moved on soon after. The neighbouring lands were those of Amalan's birth tribe, and he was keen to find his family again.

They took directions from the first village they came to, heading south-east for the coast and the Estuary Clan.

Amalan became agitated as they approached the settlement, glancing at the scenery.

"That is where I caught my first fish," he said, pointing to a rock where several small children were fishing. "And that was father's mooring for his boat." They approached a jetty, split planks rotting and broken.

"Greetings, strangers," came a cry from behind them. "Will you visit with us?"

The speaker was a short man, a spear in his hand, though he was using it as a walking stick as he hobbled towards them. "I am Varga, a herdsman of the Estuary Clan of the Poan people. Come to the village and make your introductions."

They followed Varga to the settlement, a small crowd gathering as they made for a large, central house. "We have guests," Varga shouted, stirring an old man sitting in the sun. He stood and smiled, arms extended.

"I am Isban, Chief of the Estuary clan of the Poan people. Welcome, friends."

Albyn copied his pose, arms out, palms up. "I am Albyn, spirit messenger of the Joda people, plant master, lore keeper, and healer."

Geth took her turn, smiling at the chief. "I am Geth, song keeper of the Joda people."

Both turned to Amalan, but he was scanning the crowd that had formed to see the strangers arrive.

"Mother?" he whispered.

A slender woman pushed her way to the front, mouth agape, tears streaming. "Amalan? Is it you? Where have you been? Where is your father?"

She sank to her knees in front of the boy, hugging him to her. A girl, the image of Amalan stood to one side, watching. When the woman released her grip on her son, the girl darted in, wrapping herself around Amalan.

"I thought I'd lost you," she sobbed.

"I'm here now, Garala," he said. He pulled the girl to his side and took his mother's hand.

"This is my mother, Tarvil, and my sister, Gerala," he said to Albyn and Geth. "Mother, this is Albyn, and his sister, Geth. Albyn rescued me and brought me home."

Chief Isban looked at the joyful reunion. "I think this calls for a celebration," he said. "There are stories to be told tonight."

"What of your father, Amalan?" Tarvil's eyes searched behind him, "Is he with you?"

"I'm sorry, Mother, we were attacked. They killed father and enslaved me."

Tarvil nodded her head and wiped at her tears with the back of her hand. "Then you are the man of the house, now. Ask our guests if they will do us the honour of staying in our home."

Amalan turned, realising that Albyn and Geth had heard the whole conversation.

"You honour us with your invitation, Amalan," Albyn said, bowing. "We accept."

Eight.

Amalan felt awkward under his mother's gaze, shifting on his seat. She smiled at him.

"I'm not going to stop staring at you anytime soon," she said. "I thought I'd lost you and your father. At least you came back to me."

"You have Albyn to thank for that," he said. "He drugged the Eagle Tribe and helped all the slaves escape. Most went south, but we headed north and picked up Geth before crossing to the Great Island."

"I am forever in your debt," Tarvil said, bowing to Albyn.

"I doubt our journey would have been so quick, or so easy without Amalan's help," he said.

"How is that?"

"We tried to trade the boat after we crossed from the island. I thought I was clever, getting a bag of salt for it. It seems my poor bargaining skills offended your son. He stepped in and got us weapons, a shelter, and food for our journey, then still insisted on having the bag of salt too."

"It sounds as if he is his father's son," Tarvil said. "Now, I am told there will be a feast tonight. Do you wish for food or rest before that?"

"Perhaps bread and cheese, if we may, then a rest," Albyn said, looking to Geth. She nodded her agreement.

Amalan sat with Albyn while his mother prepared the food. "Thank you for not revealing all that happened in the islands,"

Albyn said. "One day, perhaps, I may share it. I am not ashamed of the killings, but I am not proud of them."

"That is between you and the ancestors," Amalan said. "I won't reveal anything."

Two lads ran into Tarvil's house, grinning at Amalan. "Come and play, Amalan," said one.

"Thank you, no," Amalan said. "I am tired." The boys shrugged and left.

"You should go," his mother said.

"I have been gone two years," he said. His mother nodded. "Perhaps I have forgotten how to play."

Tarvil passed a platter of food to Geth, then one each to Albyn and Amalan. "I hope you will remember how to enjoy life again," she said, stroking her son's hair.

* * *

The feast that evening was followed by demands for Albyn and Geth to tell the story of their travels. They fascinated people with their walk from the very tip of the Great Island, and Geth sang them the song of the journey, listing all the landmarks they had passed.

Amalan sat between his mother and sister, saying little. He smiled at the frequent touches from both, as if to ensure he was still there.

Albyn took the lad aside as they prepared for bed. "Something is wrong, Amalan. What is it?"

"This village," he said, "It seems strange now."

"Are you not happy to have returned?"

Amalan sighed. "Two years, I was a slave to the Eagle Tribe. I was not a child, I never played, they made me work as everyone else did. You freed me from that, and on our journey, you treated me as an adult. I made fires, foraged, even hunted. You and Geth involved me in all you did."

"Do you think we were wrong in that, Amalan?" Albyn asked.

The boy stared into Albyn's eyes. "No. But now I am back home, I am supposed to be a child of eleven summers, and I don't know how."

"It would distress your mother and sister if you left again. They just got you back."

Amalan nodded. "I don't want to leave, but I don't know how to be part of the village either."

"Sleep on it," Albyn said, "We will find a solution tomorrow."

* * *

The flames crept under the thatch of the roundhouse, leaping up the dry roof, spreading into the woven willow of the walls. The smoke was thick, blinding him, choking his rapid breaths.

"Fire!" Albyn yelled, sitting up in his bed. He beat at his sleeping furs, coughing as the smoke filled his lungs.

Geth was at his side, grasping his flailing hands. "There is no fire, Albyn. It must be a dream."

Albyn fought her for a moment, then looked around. "I – I could see it – smell it. The entire house was ablaze," he said, looking around as Tarvil and her children rushed to him.

"Sit with him, Tarvil," Geth said, pushing charred wood into the embers of the fire, "I'll make some chamomile tea."

Their host sat beside him, wrapping her arms around him. She buried her face in Albyn's neck, whispering.

"It's all right, Albyn. Just a bad dream. You are safe."

He clutched her to him like a protective amulet. Guarding against the return of the horrible vision. Her slim body pressed to his, and he could catch her scent from the mane of hair under his nose.

"Thank you," Albyn said.

"I will be forever in your debt, Albyn, for the return of my son. You need never thank me."

They clutched one another until Geth returned with cups of chamomile infusion. Geth sat on Albyn's other side, sipping her drink.

"You should speak to the clan's spirit master about the fire beads," she said, "They are behind this."

"I will do it tomorrow," he said, finishing his drink. "I am sorry to have alarmed you all. We should try to sleep."

Geth, Amalan, and Garala returned to their beds. Tarvil pulled back the furs, settling Albyn, then slipped in beside him.

"I – I will be fine, Tarvil."

"I'll just lie with you until you are asleep," she said.

* * *

The first grey of dawn, filtering through the smoke hole, wakened him. Tarvil was tight to his left side, her arm across his belly. He smiled and lifted her hand, slipping from the bed. When he looked up, Amalan was standing by the hearth, watching.

"How old are you, Messenger Albyn?" he asked.

"Twenty summers. Why?"

"Mother has twenty-eight summers, it is not too big a gap, I think."

"She was just comforting me. She must have fallen asleep," Albyn said.

"You couldn't sleep either?" Amalan changed the subject. "The dawn woke me, as it always does, now."

"It will be a hard pattern to break," Albyn said. He lifted a waterskin from a peg and nodded towards the door. Amalan picked up two cups, following him outside.

They sat on a bench by the door, watching the village awake. Wood smoke hung in the still air, a woman knelt at a quern stone, grinding wheat, a baby squealed its hunger.

Chief Isban emerged from his house, sitting by the door with a steaming cup.

"Come with me," Albyn said.

Isban looked up with a smile as they approached. "Good day, Messenger Albyn, Amalan," he said, motioning for them to join him.

"Good morning, Chief Isban," Albyn replied.

"Our spirit master, Ronay, wants you to know he would welcome help from you, and your sister, while you are here," the chief said. "Will you stay with us?"

"For a while, perhaps," Albyn said. "I would be glad to help where I can. I wanted to talk to you about Amalan, though."

Isban smiled at the boy. "We are glad you're home, young man," he said.

"Since Amalan is the man of his household, now," Albyn said, "he wishes to contribute to the village, as a young warrior should."

"Oh, I don't think…" Isban began. Albyn, sitting beyond Amalan, shook his head. The chief gave an almost imperceptible nod. "Well, we have to make a trading journey to the Forest Clan. We have dried fish and salt, and need pots and leather. Would you be able to go with the trading party tomorrow, Amalan?"

The boy's face beamed. "Yes, Chief Isban, I'd be glad to. I am strong and used to long journeys."

"You wouldn't need to carry much," he said.

"I can carry a woman's load or a little more," Amalan said. "I must earn my family's place in the village."

Isban smiled. "Very well, tell my son that you will be coming, so he can organise the loads."

Amalan ran off, and Isban turned to Albyn. "You are very observant."

"He is no longer the child he appears to be. Slavery changes people."

"Indeed. Did it change you?" the chief asked.

"Forever," Albyn said.

Nine.

"You sew wounds well," Spirit Master Ronay said, as Albyn applied fresh moss to the injury and bound it with linen. "Where did you learn?"

"My teachers in the South Clan of the Joda people, then at the Bridge Clan on the Isle of Pigs."

"I travelled to the Bridge Clan as a young man," Ronay said, "Is Hafyn still chief?"

Albyn faltered in his binding of the wounded arm. "No… he died… recently."

"He was a powerful leader. Who has succeeded him?"

Albyn tied the bandage and gave instructions to the man to return in two days. "I don't know, I left before that was decided," he said.

They tidied the healing tools away and took seats by the hearth. Albyn could feel the heat of the fire stones in his pouch.

"Do you have any knowledge of powerful talismans?" he asked Ronay.

"Some. Why do you ask?"

Albyn fumbled for the necklace, placing it on the bench between them. "This. I brought it from the Isle of Pigs."

Ronay picked up the beads, scrutinising them. "The Drogga people must have thought highly of you to give you such an object."

"They had powerful feelings for me," Albyn said. "The necklace has a link to the spirit of fire. It troubles me. I don't know how to control it."

"If you wish to protect yourself from it, first wrap it in birch bark, then in red cloth. Taking it to a centre of sacred power may help too," Ronay said.

* * *

Albyn lifted the linen cloth from the pot and wrung it out. The crab-apple bark had stained it a bright red. He draped it over a bench near the fire to dry.

"I have the birch bark, Messenger Albyn," Amalan said, laying the peeled pieces on the floor.

"Is that a new axe?" Albyn asked.

"Yes, from the Forest Clan," Amalan said, testing the edge with his thumb. "I traded the knife from the Cheel People for this and a good, bone-handled blade."

Albyn chuckled. "Trader Amalan."

When the boy had gone, Albyn took out the fire beads, wrapping them in the fresh birch bark. He aired the red cloth out a little more over the embers, wrapping it around the bark package.

"Will it work?" Geth asked, setting an armful of firewood beside the hearth.

"We will find out if you will help me," he said. "Let's borrow a drum from Ronay, and we'll go to the shore."

The tide was out, and the sun was low when they settled in the soft sand. Geth gripped the crosspiece of the drum and set a slow heartbeat. Albyn made himself comfortable and closed his eyes. He raised his hand, and Geth began a fast four-beat rhythm.

Albyn travelled on the steady beat his sister kept, down into the world below. Geth drummed well but had never learned to journey as he did.

The grey sand stretched into the distance, broken only by the snaking form of the death river. The hooded figure still stood at this side of the water. Albyn stepped forward to investigate, but the wave of heat stopped him.

"Where are the fire beads?" the fire spirit said, materialising in front of him. "What have you done with them?"

Albyn smiled. "That is for me to know," he said. "I have hidden them to stop your meddling in my life."

"I will have my tribute," the spirit said. "Kneel before me."

Albyn laughed. "I will not bow to you, now get out of my way."

The scream almost deafened him as the fire spirit threw its arms wide. Flames sprang up from the sand, driving Albyn back.

"Then you shall not pass," the spirit said.

Albyn watched as the figure at the river drew back its hood and turned to face him.

"Layne!" he called, but she ignored him and stared back across the dark water once more.

Albyn lifted his hand as a signal to Geth. "Back," he said.

The sun had set, and the beach looked similar to the world he had just left. Geth laid down the drum and stood, pulling her brother to his feet.

"Did it work?"

Albyn rubbed at his eyes with the heels of his hands. "He cannot sense the beads any more, but he is preventing me from reaching the death river."

"Why would you want to go there?" Geth asked.

"There was a figure on the bank, waiting to cross," he said.

"Who?"

Albyn sighed. "Layne."

* * *

Sleep was slow to come. Albyn wondered how to get past the fire spirit and reach Layne. Something was holding her back from her ancestors, and he had to help her. A shadow crossed between him and the dying embers in the hearth. The furs lifted, and Tarvil slipped into his bed.

"For comfort," she whispered.

"Tarvil… I…"

"Just hold me, please," she said.

Albyn wrapped the woman in his arms and held her close for a while, then sighed releasing her. He sat up, pushing the furs aside, and perched on the edge of the bed.

"What is wrong?" Tarvil asked, sitting beside him, "Am I not attractive to you?"

Albyn looked up, eyes glistening in the firelight. "You are beautiful. You will make an excellent mate for some lucky man."

"But not you?"

He turned, taking her hands in his. "I was in love with a girl from the Drogga people. We were promised to each other."

"And you need to return to her?" Tarvil asked.

"She is dead," he whispered, tears falling freely now.

Tarvil's hands tightened on his. "I'm sorry."

"You deserve more than a man who will never forget another," he said. "I don't think I can ever let go of her."

Tarvil stood, stroking Albyn's wet cheek. "What was her name?"

"Layne."

Tarvil nodded, then turned and walked to her own bed.

* * *

"Albyn, look!" Geth said, pointing to a thicket close to the raspberry leaves they were harvesting.

"What?" he whispered.

"A wren. She is feeding her young."

Albyn crept closer as the parent bird flew off. Wren was his spirit animal, but he'd lost his previous companion in the rush to leave the Isle of Pigs with Layne. He peered into the nest.

"They are almost fledged," he said, backing away. "I will wait a few days, then take one. Thank you, Geth."

His sister wove him a small rush basket and, three days later, he appeared with the tiny bird captive.

"Will you be able to train it?" Geth said.

"I think so. I'll let it get used to me for a while, then I'll teach it to come back to me for food."

* * *

It was a moon later that Albyn tried to reach the death river again. The Estuary Clan had no sacred circle, so he took the fire beads, in their protective wrapping, to the tomb of the ancestors. He tucked the bundle between the stones of the low structure and went to collect Geth.

"What do you wish me to do?" Geth said, sitting beside him in the sand.

"Drum as before. I need to see if I can get to the river this time."

Geth set up the rhythm, and Albyn closed his eyes. The death river ran through the dark landscape far to his left. He turned and walked towards it. The figure stood at the water's edge once more, gazing across to the land of the dead.

"Layne!" he shouted, drawing close. He was less than twenty paces from her when the flames erupted from the sand in front of him. As the fire shimmered, Layne turned. She pushed back her hood, and Albyn saw her mouth forming shapes, but he could hear nothing.

"What do you want, Layne? Why have you not crossed to your ancestors?"

She reached up, clasping her head. Albyn wondered if she was in pain, but her face showed nothing.

"I cannot get to you. Tell me what you need?" he shouted. She shook her head, then pulled up the hood of her cloak and turned back to the river.

"Back," Albyn called, raising his hand to signal his return.

"Well?" Geth said as Albyn opened his eyes.

"The fire is still there," he said. "Layne has not crossed the river. She is trying to tell me something, but I cannot hear her voice. We needed to find a strong site, perhaps with a stone circle, that will contain the power of the beads."

"We must leave here, then?" Geth asked.

"Yes, and soon."

* * *

Spirit Master Ronay clutched Albyn to him, then turned and hugged Geth.

"Thank you for bringing Amalan back," he said. "I wish you both well in your search for a place to contain the amulet's power."

Isban came forward, his mate at his side, holding a pile of goods. The chief took a drum and beater, handing them to Geth.

"These are in appreciation of your part in returning Amalan to us," he said.

Geth held the instrument to her chest, bowing. She inspected the craftsmanship. The bent hazel hoops were tightly bound, and the well stretched skin was of deerskin rawhide. She tapped the centre, smiling at the high, bright tone. "You are too kind, Chief Isban."

The chief turned to Albyn, passing him a full hide of leather, a schist axe, and a matching knife.

"These are for you," he said.

Albyn held the gifts to his heart and bowed. He inspected the weapons. The high polish told him they were more ceremonial than practical. A valuable gift.

"Does your lore allow re-gifting?" he asked Isban.

"Of course. These are yours now," the old man said, "You may do with them as you will."

Albyn bowed, then turned to Amalan. He held the boy close, then handed him the leather.

"A warrior should have proper clothing," he said. "Perhaps your mother will make you a jerkin and leggings from this."

He hugged Garala, then Geth gave her a pretty doll she'd spent several evenings sewing. "Take care of your mother and brother," she told the small girl.

"Travel well, Albyn," Tarvil said, kissing his cheek.

"I want you to have these," Albyn said, handing her the axe and knife.

"Me. Why?"

"Because a mate of suitable status for a woman such as you may require a dowry," he said.

She held them to her chest and bowed. "Thank you."

"Perhaps I will return someday," he said.

Tarvil pressed her fingers to his lips. "You will not return this way again," she said. "but I will think of you often."

Albyn nodded and shouldered his pack. They said their final goodbyes, and headed north-west from the village.

Ten.

Geth ducked under another branch in the thick woodland. "We have missed the path somewhere," she said.

Albyn checked the position of the sun. "Yes. We're still going north, though."

There was a rustle from the thicket ahead, and Albyn stopped. He waited as something large moved towards them, pushing its way through the dense saplings growing in a small clearing. He watched a pointed head emerge and he crouched down, waving Geth to do the same.

"What is it?" she whispered.

"Bear," Albyn said. The creature reared up on its hind legs, catching their scent. It was taller than Albyn, with wicked claws extending from its massive paws. The two travellers kept still as the bear snuffled around. Albyn was sure it could see them, but it made no move to attack.

Bears and humans kept well apart. Brown bears were meat-eaters, taking fruit and roots if they were hungry. The animal gave a grunt and reared up again, walking towards Albyn and Geth. Albyn aimed his spear, knowing it was futile to try to kill the creature with just one weapon.

"When I throw this, run," he said.

"What about you?"

He drew back his arm. "Do as I say, Geth."

Geth prepared to sprint away, but as she turned, she caught a movement in the bushes.

The bear roared, and when Geth looked back, two arrows hung from its flank. Another shaft whizzed into its neck as it lumbered at Albyn.

"Run," he said, casting the short spear at the raging animal.

Geth stood frozen as Albyn's throw hit true, and the flint head pierced the thick fur of its throat. Two men ran from the bushes, falling upon the wounded creature as it dropped just paces from Albyn. One man straddled the animal's back, pulling the enormous head up, while the other plunged a knife alongside Albyn's spear.

The bear struggled for a moment, then gave a final groan as blood pooled on the forest floor.

"I thought I was going to die," Albyn said.

The red-faced man with the knife stood and wiped blood from his eyes. "It would have killed you in a moment," he said.

The second man released the limp head of the bear and stood. "I am Kenna of the Lake Clan of the Atay people," he said. "This is my brother, Den."

"I am Albyn, a spirit messenger of the South Clan of the Joda Tribe. This is my sister, Geth, a song keeper. Is it not unusual for a bear to attack people?"

Den turned away, covering his face with bloody hands.

"It is a killer," Kenna said. "Two days ago, it came to the edge of our village. Den's daughter was playing with some other children. It killed her with a swipe of its paw, then dragged her away. Her name was Kira, she had three summers."

Geth rushed forward, taking the hands of the bereaved father, whispering to him.

"How far is it to your village?" Albyn asked.

"Two days," Kenna said. "The bear has not paused day or night since we began trailing it. We vowed to kill it."

"Too far to take it back," Albyn said. "I can do a ceremony for the child to placate the ancestors for her death. I do not know your customs, but it is what my tribe would do."

Den looked up, tears drawing lines through the blood on his cheeks. "Do what you need to do, Spirit Messenger," he said.

"Will you take the skin?" Albyn asked. "We need to cut out its heart for the ceremony."

"We want no part of it," Den said, "Take what you will. Without your spear, we may still be tracking it."

Albyn took his knife and set about skinning the bear. Geth patted Den on the back, then joined her brother in the grim task. They rolled the hide, then Albyn broke open the rib cage, extracting the heart.

"We will need a good fire," he said. "can you take care of that while I prepare?"

Den got out a fire-bow, while Kenna collected wood. They soon had a blaze going and watched while Albyn cleansed himself in a stream nearby.

Geth took her drum and sat close to the fire. The brothers sat back a little, as Albyn held the heart in both hands and sat at the fire. He nodded to his sister, and she began the beat that would carry him below.

Albyn headed straight for the death river, the bear's heart clutched in his hand. Twenty paces from the water, the flame sprang from the sand, halting him.

"Where are you, spirit of fire?" he called. There was a whispering in the air, and the face of the spirit appeared, glowing red in the dim light.

"Who summons me?" he asked.

"Do you forget so soon?" Albyn asked. "I need to pass to the river."

"Where are my beads?" the spirit said. "Where is my tribute?"

Albyn cupped the heart in both hands, offering it to the fire spirit. "See. The heart of a bear. An offering to you." He tossed the heart into the flames, watching it sizzle and char until nothing remained. As the fire died, Albyn walked to the river.

"Ancestors that love me bring the spirit of the child, Kira."

The air across the river shimmered and solidified into two figures, one old, the other a small child. The child still bore the scars of her death, and Albyn wondered how long spirits took to heal after crossing the river.

"Kira. I bring greetings from your father, Den, and your uncle, Kenna. They wish you to know that they have avenged you against the creature that took your life. Its heart was accepted by the spirits as an offering. You may watch over those that love you, through the fire, when you wish. Go now, with your ancestor, and be at peace."

The child's scarred face smiled as she clutched the hand of the elder. He bowed as they turned from the water, fading into the dim light.

"What did you do?" the fire spirit asked, stopping him as he turned from the river.

"What I have always done with earth, air, or water. You accepted an offering as an exchange, so one taken too soon could have access to those they love. If they drowned or were lost at sea, I would make the bargain with the waters, likewise for those lost to the earth or those sky-buried, with the air."

"None have ever made this pact with me," the fire spirit said.

Albyn smiled. "You accepted the tribute."

"That was a tribute to me, as your master!" the spirit said.

"Everything comes at a cost. Will you break the bargain?"

The spirit faded, "Begone," it said.

Albyn raised his arm. "Back," he called.

"Is it done?" Geth asked as she set the drum aside.

Albyn looked at the fire. There was no trace of the bear's heart left. "He has accepted the tribute," Albyn said. "Den, Kenna, look for her in the flames, in the embers. In time, she may learn to speak through the fire. She will be with you, watching."

Though such displays were only seen in the closest of friends, Den pulled Albyn to his feet and hugged him.

"Thank you, Messenger. I am in your debt."

The tearful man sat close to the dying fire, then, whispering to his lost child.

"We should make camp," Albyn said to Kenna. "We'll travel with you to your village tomorrow if you have no objections."

"They will welcome you," he said. "Kira's mother will want to thank you, and our spirit master will wish to speak with you about the deal with the fire spirit."

"Did you see Layne?" Geth asked as they erected their shelter.

Albyn shook his head. "The journey was focussed on the child. I saw no one else."

* * *

Two days later, they walked into the Lake Clan village. Word soon spread that the death of Kira had been avenged, and the tribe's young spirit master came to visit Den's home.

"I am Shalin, spirit master of my people. They tell me you have made a pact with the spirit of fire," he said, holding out his hands in welcome.

"I am Albyn, a spirit messenger of the Joda tribe. Yes, I made the bargain. Your ways may not be mine, but something needed to be done. I did not intend to offend."

"I have made similar deals with the spirit of water, but have never dared to work with the fire spirit," Shalin said. "Are you a fire master?"

Albyn looked up at the mention of the fire masters. "No, but I have an artefact sacred to them. It came to me after its owner's death."

"The fire masters are legend. I do not know of any that survive, hereabouts."

"Kira's family is glad to have the link to her spirit," Albyn said. "Perhaps my sister and I could stay until you inter her bones?"

"You will be welcome," Shalin said.

* * *

Geth spent many days working on the bearskin, scraping, washing and tanning. She had taken the creature's fangs, and Albyn drilled them, threading them onto a cord to wear around his neck.

When Spirit Master Shalin deemed Kira's bones to be ready, they were taken down from the sky-burial platform and placed in a basket. The entire clan gathered at dusk as they carried the remains to the long tomb. Shalin crawled in through the narrow passageway, Albyn following with a torch. They laid the child to rest in a niche on the west side.

There was a solemn silence, then Geth took her drum and sang a song of remembrance for the girl. The villagers returned to the settlement, standing, talking around the central fire.

"She will be at peace now," Albyn said to Geth, "The song was very moving, people liked it."

All heads turned at the scream from the fireside. Kira's mother knelt by the embers, tears flowing.

"I see her. Look!"

Albyn rushed to the fire, staring over the woman's shoulder. There, in the glowing coals, he could make out the face of a girl. A gust of wind fanned the fire, and the mouth curled into a smile.

Eleven.

The leaves were turning to gold and red, carpeting the paths, as they travelled further north. The Lake Clan had been generous on their departure, giving gifts of food and flints, boots for Geth and a carved stone ball for Albyn.

"Did Shalin say how far to this stone circle he spoke of?" Geth asked.

"We should be there tomorrow," Albyn said.

Geth sang the song of their journey, reminding herself of the main landmarks along their way. "Short of the great estuary, if my song is right," she said.

"Your songs are always right, Geth. You are an accomplished song keeper."

They bedded down in a sheltered valley that night and, early next day, found themselves at a small circle of stones.

"Greetings," Albyn called to a short man who appeared to be tending the site.

"Who are you?" the man asked.

"I am Albyn, a spirit messenger of the Joda people. This is my sister, Geth, a song keeper."

"What do you want?"

Albyn was close enough to see messenger tattoos around the man's right eye, now. He was taken aback that he had still made no attempt to introduce himself.

"We are travellers. We wish to make use of your sacred site," Albyn said.

"No. That will not be possible. This is the site of the North Boat Clan. It is for our use only."

Albyn turned to Geth, who shrugged. No tribe, or clan, should ever prevent travellers from accessing sacred sites. It was the lore of all the peoples.

Albyn kept his hands extended. "What is your name? We have travelled from the Lake Clan. Are we still in Atay lands?"

The man extended his own hands in a grudging welcome. "I am Groel, Spirit Messenger of the North Boat Clan of the Atay people." He stretched his name into two syllables, and Albyn struggled to place his accent. It was not Atay. Albyn's wren chose that moment to alight on his shoulder, and he turned, smiling at the bird.

"Is that your spirit animal?" Groel asked.

"Yes," Albyn said, "What is yours?" He hoped to find some way to placate this hostile man and see if these stones had enough power to shield the fire beads.

"My creature is the bear," Groel said, "An animal of significant power."

"Well, I may have a suitable gift for you, Groel," Albyn said, reaching to slip off the thong around his neck. "These are the teeth of a great brown bear, and we would be glad for a powerful messenger like you to have them."

Geth smiled to herself. She had known all the young women Albyn had shown an interest in, and all had said he had a tongue of honey.

Groel stood dumbfounded for a moment before reaching over to take the necklace from Albyn's hand.

"You are most generous, Messenger. Perhaps you would like to come to meet our chief?"

The two travellers grinned at each other as Groel led them off towards a cluster of houses beyond a field of ripe barley. The village was small but well cared for. Children played around the houses, and there was an air of busyness about the place.

Groel disappeared into a house, emerging moments later with a tall, sharp-featured woman. She smiled and greeted the siblings.

"Welcome. I am Rosh, chief of the North Boat Clan. We are glad to have you visit us."

Albyn smiled at the pleasant reception and introduced himself and Geth.

"Joda Tribe?" Rosh said. "Do you plan to return there?"

"Not straight away. Why?"

"We have heard that war has broken out between the Isle of the Eagles and the Isle of Pigs. Each claims the other has stolen sacred artefacts. It will be unsafe to travel there until they resolve it."

Albyn's hand drifted to his pouch. "Then we shall continue our travels elsewhere for a while," he said.

"Groel tells me you wish to use our circle of stones. May I ask what for?"

"A loved one died, in tragic circumstances," Albyn said. "I fear she has not crossed the river, so I seek a powerful site to work with her spirit."

"How can that be?" Groel said. "Why has she not been able to cross the river?"

"That's what we wish to find out," Albyn smiled. The Atay messenger was annoying him, but he could not, now, mention the fire beads for fear someone this far north had travelled to the Isle of Pigs and knew of them.

"Come in," Rosh said. "We shall feed you and try to help your quest."

Rosh served them a meal of lean beef, cheese, and bread, foods of the best quality. Albyn suspected that she was glad for them to visit, even if her spirit messenger was not.

"Have we offended Groel?" Geth asked when the messenger excused himself from their meeting.

"No, not that I know of," Rosh said. "He comes from the Doran peoples to the east, they are less trusting than ourselves."

"Barley grows on flattest land, and stones lie down that ought to stand," Geth recited.

"You have visited the Doran?" Rosh asked.

"No. It is part of the journey song if we were to travel there," Geth said. "I do not understand the reference to stones."

"They often have stones in their circles set on edge, rather than on end. Our old spirit master used to say they were too lazy to lift them." She glanced at the door. "Don't tell Groel that," she whispered.

Geth and Albyn laughed. "May we stay tonight, Chief Rosh?" Albyn asked. "We will make use of your circle tomorrow, then be on our way."

"Stay as long as you wish," Rosh said. "Please stay in my house. I have no mate, and Groel's house is small."

"Thank you," Albyn said.

* * *

After breakfast next day, Albyn and Geth made their way to the stones. Groel had seemed irritated that they didn't want his help, but he didn't insist on accompanying them.

Geth took out her drum, while Albyn retrieved the fire beads. He set them inside the circle, tight against the north stone. If he could hide them anywhere, it would be in the place of earth, the densest element and the stone furthest from the place of fire in the south.

He sat facing south, in the centre of the ring, then nodded to Geth. She set up a steady beat, and Albyn closed his eyes.

The hooded figure stood staring at the river. Albyn walked forward, stepping with care as he got closer.

Not five paces from the figure, the flames burst from the ground, driving him back.

"Layne," he called. The figure turned, her small hand pulling off her hood. She smiled, but there was no joy there.

"Why do you not cross?" he asked.

She reached up, holding her head.

"Are you in pain? Can you not speak?"

She shook her head, then pointed across the dark waters.

"I know what you want, Layne, but I don't know how to help you. Tell me what I must do."

Layne shook her head, then pulled up her hood and turned back to the river.

"Back," Albyn said, raising his arm.

"Well?" Geth asked as he opened his eyes.

"She is still there. She holds her head but is not in pain. I know she wishes to cross to the land of the dead but seems unable to go. I cannot get her to speak. Perhaps she can't."

"What do we do now?" Geth asked.

"I don't know," he said. "The fire still prevents me from reaching her. Somewhere with greater power than here, perhaps? I cannot ask Groel for fear he knows of the fire beads. You heard what Rosh said about a war."

"That is your doing," Geth said. "You took those beads and the eagle amulet. You must return them to their owners, Albyn."

"No. Hafyn left his own daughter in slavery, and she died because of it. The Eagle Tribe took us prisoner, for no reason, then treated us like animals. Their poor building work caused Layne's death. They all deserve what they get."

Geth nodded as Albyn retrieved the fire beads. "So, where do we go?"

"Let's ask Rosh."

* * *

"There are a few places of greater power in these lands," Rosh said when they were seated with drinks. "The greatest, though, is far to the west. Have you heard of the Long Islands?"

Geth closed her eyes.

"Far to the west, a long strip of land.

Over the sea, great circles do stand.

Yorvyn, the giant, in all of his might,

Raised them up in the space of a night."

"Is this the journey song for the Long Islands?" Albyn asked.

"Yes," Geth said frowning. "I must remember the rest if we are to travel there."

"Head west from here," Rosh said, "There is an obvious track, and the Atay people will keep you on the right path. The place you seek is called Classac."

"We are most grateful, Rosh," Geth said. She reached for a bundle beside her belongings. Albyn nodded when her gaze met his. "We would like to make you a gift of this skin."

"Is that…"

"Bear," Albyn said. "It attacked us, and we had cause to kill it. We would like you to have it, in recognition of your help."

"It is well cured," Rosh said, running her fingers through the thick fur. "Did you do this, Geth?"

"I learned a little from the Poan people," she said.

Rosh inspected the skin side. "You learned a lot." She clutched it to her heart with her left hand and bowed. "I am honoured. Thank you."

"We will leave in the morning," Albyn said.

Rosh smiled. "And we will provision you for your journey."

Twelve.

It took five days to reach the west coast, and another day to walk the length of the spit of land that pointed out into the ocean. They had stayed with Atay clans on all but one night and had passed messages and gifts along as they travelled. It was late afternoon when they reached the Shore Clan.

Albyn and Geth asked for the clan's chief, and a couple led them to the main house.

"Greetings," the old man said, stepping outside. "I am Bartev, chief of the Shore Clan." He beckoned to a young woman, about Albyn's age. "And this is our new spirit messenger, Tarna. She comes to us from the Cheel people."

Albyn and Geth gave their status and bowed to the chief and Tarna.

"We seek a crossing to the Long Islands. Will you be able to help us?"

"It is late. Please accept our hospitality for tonight, and I will speak with our boatmen in the morning. Tarna, will you take care of our guests?"

* * *

The house of the protected-of-spirit was new. The thatch was golden in the sunset, and fresh shavings still lay around the mud daubed walls.

"Your house is beautiful," Geth said.

"It was one of my demands." Tarna waved them to seats beside the fire, then shouted out of the door.

"Genna. Bring firewood in."

"Demands?" Albyn said. "What do you mean?"

A girl of seven or eight came in, laden with sticks. She made up the fire, then heated water.

"I became a spirit messenger at the summer solstice," Tarna said. "I could have gone north, to a clan of my own people, but the Shore Clan had been without the protection of spirit for many moons. They asked how they could persuade me to come and live here."

"So, a new house?" Geth said.

"The old house was falling apart. It lay in a dip and was always damp. I asked for a new house, and that they accept Genna along with me."

"Is she your sister?" Albyn asked.

"No. Her parents both died of a sickness of the lungs last winter. My old spirit master put her into my care. When I said I was leaving, she was so troubled, I had to take her with me."

"Will you apprentice?" Geth asked the girl.

"Yes. Messenger Tarna has promised it at the winter solstice."

"Serve us tea, please, Genna," Tarna said, "I will make our food soon."

* * *

Bartev found the two travellers at breakfast the next morning.

"We have a boat leaving in three days, if the weather holds," he said. "You could travel to the Long Islands then if we can agree on some compensation."

Albyn smiled. "Of course, Chief Bartev. We will take valuable cargo space." He reached into his pack, pulling out the stone ball from the North Boat Clan. Bartev's eyes widened as Albyn passed him the intricate carving.

"This is from the east coast," Bartev said. "It is beautiful, but it is too much."

"Nonsense," Albyn said. "Feed and house us until the boat sails. It is a good trade."

* * *

It was their last morning, and Albyn had taken all their belongings to the shore. When he returned, Tarna was waiting for him.

"Are the Long Islands your last destination?" she asked.

"I don't know. Why do you ask?"

Tarna smiled. "I am looking for a mate. You are handsome enough, and I think I am not ugly. Would you consider a bonding?"

"We don't know each other, Tarna. I was promised to another… but she was taken from me too soon. I'm not ready to make that commitment to anyone else."

"That's a shame," she said. "Remember me, if you change your mind. Travel well, Albyn."

"Thank you. Geth and I appreciate your hospitality." Albyn held her for a moment, uncomfortable after her offer. "Goodbye, Tarna."

* * *

"Bonding?" Geth shrieked. "She has known you for three days."

"Yes," Albyn said. "I was unsure of what to say to her."

"I mean, she is good looking." Geth grinned, "You didn't… comfort her?"

Albyn blushed. "No."

"You comforted Amalan's mother, Tarvil. I thought you might stay with her."

"Tarvil was grieving her mate, and neither of us made any promises. Our relationship was not physical."

Geth thought she saw a tear in her brother's eye, but he turned away, calling to the boatman.

"When will we arrive on the Long Islands?"

"That's the bay, there," the sailor said. "We'll be ashore by noon."

Albyn could see a cluster of houses above the shore and a group of people making for the beach as they drew closer.

"That's the Boat Clan of the Tribe of the South," their boatman said. "The wind is changing. If you help us unload, and load the trade goods, I can return today."

"We'll be happy to help," Albyn said, as the boat crunched into the shingle beach.

There were plenty of hands ready to assist, and they exchanged flints and salt beef, pottery and grain, for soft leather, polished stone axes, and a litter of live piglets.

When they were done, they waved the boat off and sat for a moment.

"Greetings," said a young woman. Albyn recognised the tattoos of a spirit messenger, though the pattern differed from his own. "Our chief has asked me to take you to my house. I am Shenag, Spirit Messenger of the Boat Clan of the Tribe of the South."

Geth and Albyn introduced themselves and followed the woman to her home. They found out a little about the islands, but were tired from the loading and, soon after they'd eaten an evening meal, excused themselves to bed.

* * *

Just after sunrise the next morning, they were heading north. Shenag told them that the place they sought, Classac, was only two days distant. She said she visited often, and the complex arrangement of stones held great power.

They slept in their shelter the first night, nestled in a valley beneath a great mountain. There were no villages on their route, and the animals seemed unbothered by their presence. Sitting by their fire, as the dusk drew in, they watched a dozen red deer trot past. Shortly after, a pack of wolves made their way along the valley, single file. Albyn wondered if one of the older deer would make their meal that night.

Towards the end of the second day, they spotted the jagged silhouette of the stones atop a hill ahead of them.

"They are huge," Geth said. "They stretch across the whole hilltop."

"I hope this circle will have power enough to hide the fire beads from the spirit," Albyn said. "Come on, let's see if they are friendly."

* * *

There was a warm welcome and, after introductions, Dagreth, the chief, showed them to the spirit messenger's house.

"Please make yourselves comfortable here," he said. "Our spirit messenger died at sea four moons since. We'd be grateful if you would help us with our sick for a while."

"I'd be happy to," Albyn said, looking around the house.

"Nothing has been touched in here," Dagreth said. "Please use anything you need. Someone will bring you food and a water skin soon."

"Will this circle be strong enough?" Geth asked when the leader had gone.

"We'll find out tomorrow," Albyn said. "Now give me a hand and let's get the fire lit."

* * *

Albyn opened the door of the roundhouse and gave a high, chirring whistle. Moments later, his wren fluttered to his shoulder. He'd carried the bird in a grass basket while they travelled, freeing her each night to feed at dusk and dawn. He turned over a rock beside the door, and the tiny bird flashed to the ground, picking at the beetles he'd exposed.

Geth was still sleeping, so he raked through the ashes of the fire, blowing it back to life with some fresh kindling.

"Good morning," Geth said, pulling on her clothes. "What are we going to do today?"

"Well, Dagreth mentioned some healing work," Albyn said. "Let's eat, then we'll see what he has for me."

Geth inspected the thinning soles of her boots, then pulled them on. "There's bread left, and a little meat," she said, as Albyn dropped hot stones into a pot of water.

Their meal finished, Albyn sought the chief, who directed him to an old woman, crippled with swollen joints. He promised her he'd find plants to treat her later that day, then returned to the spirit messenger's house.

Two people were waiting at the door.

"Will you look at my wound, Messenger," said a man, holding up a bandaged arm. "It itches so much."

Albyn removed the binding, finding a healed wound bearing three coarse, loose stitches. It would scar, but it was too late to do anything more. He cut away the stitches, then washed the arm.

"Someone should have done that days ago," he said, "but no harm. You may leave it uncovered now."

The man bowed and presented Albyn with a small joint of beef wrapped in dock leaves.

"Is it your custom to give gifts to healers?" he asked.

"Yes, Messenger, such as each person can spare."

"Then, thank you."

The second person at the door was a girl of ten summers. She bowed to Albyn, then Geth, as she entered the house.

"Grandfather has sent me to assist you," she said. "I am to fetch wood and water, tend your fire, and cook if you need me to."

"Grandfather?" Albyn asked.

"Chief Dagreth," she explained.

"Very well. I am Messenger Albyn, my sister is Song Keeper Geth."

"My name is Lanis," she said, glancing at the hearth. "I will fetch firewood for you."

Thirteen.

There was a chill in the air as Albyn and Geth climbed the hill to the sacred stones. Lanis had stewed the beef and made fresh bread for their meal, and they were glad of the hot food in their bellies as the wind danced around the Classac stones.

Albyn wandered around the circle, trailing fingers across the grey rocks. "I'd love to connect with these stones," he said. "I can feel the power in them from touching them."

Geth glanced at the western sky. "Make the drum journey," she said, "the daylight will not last much longer."

Albyn placed the red-wrapped fire beads next to the northernmost stone, then settled himself in the circle's centre. Geth sat to his left, the drum in her lap. He nodded to his sister and closed his eyes as she set up a fast four-beat.

The death river surged amongst blackened rocks not twenty paces in front of him. The solitary figure of Layne stood at the water's edge. Albyn shuffled forward, waiting for the fire spirit's barrier to flare from the grey sand. Nothing happened.

"Layne?" he said as he approached her. She turned, pushing back the hood of her cloak. "I have got to you at last. I miss you so much, my love."

A sad smile flickered across her mouth. She raised her hand, pointing across the fast-flowing waters.

"I know. You wish to be with your ancestors. I don't know why you cannot cross, Layne."

She clutched at her head, as before, eyes pleading with him to understand. She pointed to her body, then at the raging waters.

"You, in the water?" She nodded. "I surrendered your bones to the sea," Albyn said, "I could not save them. Only your skull."

Layne's spirit nodded again, pointing to her head. Then the water.

"Do I need to give your skull to the sea as well?" he asked.

Layne smiled for the first time. She mimed taking her head and placing it in the waters of the river.

"This will free you, your remains being in one place, even if that place is the ocean? Layne, is this why you cannot speak?"

The smile melted away. She nodded, and Albyn could see a tear on her cheek.

"I will do it tomorrow," he said. "Please, wait for me to return before you go to your ancestors."

Layne raised her hand in farewell. Pulling her hood over her head, she turned back to the river once more.

"Back," Albyn said, raising his hand to signal Geth.

"Well, has she crossed?" Geth asked.

"No, but I know why, now," Albyn said. "I told you I saved her skull from being washed away by the sea?"

"Yes."

"I need to give it to the sea too, so her remains are reunited. Then she will join her ancestors."

"Tomorrow," Geth said as the sun slipped below the horizon.

* * *

Albyn stood close to the foaming surf, clutching the skull of the woman he loved. He kissed it, closing his eyes and seeing her sparkling hazel gaze in his memory. He placed it at the surf's edge, watching as the next wave rolled the head towards him, then sucked it into the foam. He waited a moment, then sat on the damp sand.

The tinkle of the lapping waves reminded him of Layne's contagious giggle, and he smiled despite his grief. He gazed into the frothing water, hoping to see some semblance of her there.

"How will I live without you, Layne?" he whispered. "We were going to be together, you and me."

"She is whole again?" Geth asked, sitting beside him

Albyn rubbed at reddened eyes and nodded. "If only I'd let the sea take all of her after her death," he said.

"All things happen for a reason, Albyn. She has led us to a sacred place that can contain the power of the fire beads. Come on, we'll go to the stone circle so you can bid her goodbye."

They collected Geth's drum from the house, then walked up the hill to the Classac circle. Albyn tucked the fire beads beside the north stone and sat with his sister. Geth set the rhythm, and he closed his eyes.

Layne was right in front of him when he opened his eyes in the lower world. She smiled.

"Thank you, Albyn. I can cross to my ancestors now."

"Perhaps I can come with you," he said.

"No, you must remain with the living. It is not your time to die," Layne said.

"But it was your time?"

She shook her head. "No, but I was taken, and there is no undoing it. Please do not follow me. Promise it."

Tears streamed down Albyn's cheeks as he looked into the face he loved. "I promise I will wait until the ancestors call me. But I will miss you with every breath I take, until then."

"I will miss you too." Layne looked across the river where a woman waited. *"May I hold him one last time?"*

"You have not crossed the death river, we will allow one touch," the figure said.

Layne flung her arms around Albyn's neck as he clutched her waist, pulling her close. Their lips met, his warm and vital, hers cold as stone.

"I will be here, waiting," she whispered. *"Years from now, we will be together, and we will have all of time in the land across the river."*

"I shall wish for it every day," Albyn said.

"I cannot stay," Layne whispered. *They parted, stepping back until just their fingertips touched.*

"I love you," she said. *"Look for me in the waves at the shore."*

"I love you, Layne, forever."

He watched her step into the turbulent waters, seeming to float across to the ancestor that waited for her. She turned one last time, waving as she dissolved into the air.

"Return the fire beads," came a voice from across the river. *Albyn looked up to find Hafyn, Layne's father, the man he'd murdered, glaring at him.*

"Why should I?"

"Men are dying because of your actions," Hafyn said.

Albyn stepped to the water's edge. "No, men are dying because you disowned your daughter, because you failed to take her away from the Eagle Tribe. Men are dying because you denied your own flesh and condemned her to beatings and starvation, and to her death."

"I did not know!" Hafyn screamed.

"You did not care!"

"I beg you, save the people of the Drogga."

"Let them all die, every one, and let their spirits come to you for an explanation. What will you tell them, Hafyn? What will you tell Layne?"

"She will now acknowledge me," Hafyn sobbed. "I have tried to speak with her spirit, but she turns away."

"I will suffer for all of my life without her," Albyn said. "May you suffer likewise, for all of time."

He turned from the river, raised his hand and called out, "Back."

Albyn's eyes opened, and he looked around him, disoriented.

"You were gone a long time," Geth said. "It worried me."

"She has crossed to the land of the dead," he said. "She is at peace."

Albyn took the fire beads from the north stone and walked from the circle. He went to a rocky outcrop, to the south, and reached into a crevice, placing the red-wrapped package deep inside.

"There, let the fire spirit find them now," he said.

"Spirit Messenger Albyn! Come quickly." Lanis came running up the path to the stones, gasping for breath. She stopped, bent over for a moment. "Father was mending the roof and fell off. I cannot wake him."

Fourteen.

Albyn rushed into the house, finding Lanis' father, Chay, laid on a bed. He checked for breathing, then looked for any significant blood loss.

"Lanis, heat water. We need to clean your father up," he said. "Geth, fetch my tool pouch."

Chay's left ear was battered, showing he'd landed on that side. Albyn stroked his fingers through the man's hair, searching for a telltale bump on his skull. What he found made him shudder. A few finger breadths above the left ear, under the skin, was a hollow.

"His skull is broken," Albyn announced, not looking up.

"Will he die?" Dagreth asked, kneeling beside the bed.

"If he is bleeding, inside his head, it is likely."

"Can nothing be done?" Lanis asked. Her eyes were wet as she brought the scalding water to Albyn's side.

Albyn glanced at Geth as she opened his tool pouch and spread it on a table. "It is possible to cut a hole in the skull to allow the bad spirit, that has attacked his brain, to leave. I have seen it done once," he said.

Geth caught his eye, and he shrugged. She had been there when their own spirit master had performed the operation on a man with a broken skull. He had died despite the attempt.

"If it may help him, do it," Dagreth said. "Now, everyone outside. Leave Albyn and his sister to help my son."

The small crowd of villagers left, chased by their chief. Lanis looked up at Albyn.

"May I stay?"

"If you can stomach this kind of work, it would be useful to have another helper," he said, reaching for a flint blade.

Albyn shaved the hair from the site of the damage, then muttered a prayer to the ancestors before cutting through Chay's scalp. Geth held back the flap of skin, while Albyn patted at the pooling blood. There was a dent in Chay's skull, and the bone was cracked. He took a new flint burin and scraped at the bone. He cut deep lines in a square shape, bigger than the damage, wearing through the bone.

Geth held the head steady while Lanis rinsed the cloths in hot water to mop up the blood.

Albyn sighed as the square of shattered bone fell free. He lifted the pieces out, then mopped at the blackening clot he found inside. Satisfied that he'd removed all the loose bone, he pulled the flap of skin back into place and reached for the needle. Once he'd pierced holes in the skin, Lanis passed him pieces of pounded sinew. He threaded them through the holes, tying them tightly.

Albyn had placed thirty tiny stitches before he was satisfied. He washed the wound once more, patted it dry, and applied honey. Geth was busy with bandaging Chay's head as Albyn stretched his stiff legs and stood.

"Fetch your grandfather," he said to Lanis.

"Are you alright?" Geth asked. "The day is gone, it is near dark outside."

Albyn nodded, rubbing at his neck with bloodied hands. He turned as Dagreth came in.

"Well?"

"I have done all I can," Albyn said. "The cutting went well. The wound is closed and dressed. All we can do now is ask for the ancestors' help."

Dagreth nodded as Lanis appeared with a cup of water. Albyn drank it down, then asked for another.

"We have bread and cheese," the girl said, checking the shelf for leftovers.

"Nonsense," Dagreth said, "Go to my house, my mate will feed you and Geth. Lanis and I will watch over Chay."

* * *

Albyn sat on the beach, watching the foaming surf, listening to the rush and draw of the waves. Sometimes, he fancied he could see Layne's face in the foam, could hear the tinkle of her laughter in the splash of water.

The hand on his shoulder startled him. Geth stroked his hair from his eyes. "Did you sleep at all?" she said.

"A little. I watched him most of the night. Is there any change?"

Geth shook her head. "Lanis is with him. His breathing is steady, but he is too hot. Come and eat."

They made their way back to the house, and Albyn checked on Chay before eating a little bread. Lanis came over and hugged him, and he stroked the girl's hair.

"Thank you for doing what you could," she said.

Albyn left the women with Chay and walked up to the stone circle. He sat with his back to the north stone, soaking up the energy, closing his eyes and drifting off.

When he woke, the sun was high in the sky. He looked around, finding Lanis standing at the edge of the circle.

"What's wrong?" he asked, dreading the worst.

"Father had opened his eyes, but his speech makes no sense. Has a spirit possessed him?"

Albyn stood and took the girl's hand. "Come with me, and we'll see," he said.

* * *

There was fear in Chay's eyes when Albyn got back to the house. He sat beside the man and took his hand.

"I am Albyn, do you remember me?" he asked.

"Ess," Chay said.

"Are you in pain?"

"Aaa yed."

"Your head took a grave blow when you fell. We will get you willow bark tea," Albyn said.

"Blows to the head can have many effects," he said to Lanis. "Can you make the tea for him?"

The girl nodded and raked stones from the fire.

After a drink, Chay drifted back to sleep, and Albyn visited Dagreth.

"His speech is poor, an effect of the bad spirits," he told the chief. "I will watch him for a few days. If nothing is any worse, he may recover."

"Thank you, Albyn. We are in your debt," Dagreth said.

Albyn sat at the bedside, drum in hand, for the next two days. He drummed for Chay's spirit, often going to the lower world to check if he was waiting to cross.

When Chay awakened, he was impossible to understand, ranting in words no one could make out. Sweat poured from his body for half the day, then he shivered with cold into the evening. Exhaustion took Albyn at the end of the second day, and Geth took over the vigil.

* * *

No one was more surprised than Albyn when, at the end of the following day, Chay could sit up and speak to his mate with little more than a slight slur to his speech. When he was able to stand the next morning, Albyn declared the bad spirits had left his body.

After the constant stress of the last days, Albyn slept half the day away, then took himself off to the shore. He was sitting watching the waves when footsteps in the shingle roused him.

"May I sit with you?" Dagreth asked.

"Please do," Albyn said.

"Thank you for saving my son," he said. "You are a talented healer. I wanted to ask if you would stay. We need someone such as you to be the guardian of our sacred stones, and care for our people."

Albyn stroked his chin. "It would depend on how Geth felt," he said. "I abandoned her once before. I would need to know if she wanted to stay here too."

"Perhaps you should look over there," Dagreth said, pointing along the beach. Geth was walking, hand-in-hand with the young man whose arm Albyn had treated on their first day. Geth laughed at something her companion said, then looked up, waving to Albyn. He waved back.

"Will he be good to her?"

"Denny is my nephew, a strong warrior, and an expert hunter. He already has two cows of his own."

"I will speak to Geth, if she is happy here, we will stay," Albyn said.

"If you stay," Dagreth said. "Lanis asks if you will take her as your apprentice?"

Albyn nodded. "We shall see," he said.

The end.

Get your free book!

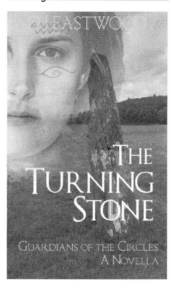

The twin girls that Spirit Messenger Yalta has carried in her belly for so many months come too soon… born dead. She'd hoped that their birth would prompt a proposal of bonding from her lover, Galcar, but he ridicules her for not being able to carry his children.

She runs from her home village in shame, walking the countryside, racked with guilt and tormented by fevers.

When the fever breaks, she has been taken is by Treith, Spirit Master of the great stones of Stanna.

She makes a home there, but the power of the stone circle is failing, and less people come to the solstice gatherings each year. Soon there will not be enough to reposition the turning stone, and change the seasons.

When Treith dies, Yalta is left in charge of the sacred site, and when just a handful of people trickle in to celebrate the solstice, one of them is Galcar, determined to ridicule her once more.

Will she be forced to depart in shame again, or can Yalta rebuild the power of Stanna, and take control of the turning stone?

Go to www.apprenticetattoo.co.uk for more details.

Printed in Great Britain
by Amazon

56613918R00052